NO LONGER
SEATTLE P

D0179727

Angel Rock Leap

Ellen Weisberg
and
Ken Yoffe

WALDORF PUBLISHING

Published by Waldorf Publishing
2140 Hall Johnson Road
#102-345
Grapevine, Texas 76051
www.WaldorfPublishing.com

Angel Rock Leap

ISBN: 978-1-943849-87-1
Library of Congress Control Number: 2015957006

Copyright © 2018

All rights reserved. No part of this book may be reproduced
or transmitted in any form or by any means whatsoever
without express written permission from the author, except
in the case of brief quotations embodied in critical articles
and reviews. Please refer all pertinent questions to the
publisher. All rights reserved. No part of this book may
be reproduced or transmitted in any form or by any means,
electronic or mechanical, including photocopying,
recording, or by an information storage and retrieval
system except by a reviewer who may quote brief passages
in a review to be printed in a magazine or newspaper
without permission in writing from the publisher.

Dedication

To Poppy Joe and Nana Sheila

Chapter 1

I crossed my legs and clutched the edges of a photocopied textbook chapter on my lap. I needed to focus. I lifted one thigh off of the other, set my feet hard and flat on the floor, and began curling the corners of the manuscript in such a way that they resembled rolling waves of sea water.

For a brief moment, I felt calm.

Dr. Weinstein busied himself with some papers in his briefcase and, with a bored expression, took a sip of coffee and sat across from me. He had dark folds under his eyes from what I assumed was an accumulation of decades of sleep deprivation and obsessive compulsion. He was a stereotype: the average research scientist, overwrought with ambition, overflowing with ideas, and dreadfully overtired.

"Sarah," he said, lifting his heavy brow.

I stared down at my manhandled pages.

"Your midterm scores came in." He pinched his lips together with his fingers.

I shifted uneasily, swallowing hard. "I know," I said. "I received them last week."

"You passed one out of four," he said, still looking bored. "It was for the English class that we require all the pharmaceutical science undergrads to take to make sure they can read and write halfway decently. You failed biochemistry, cell biology, and statistics."

I squared my shoulders. "OK. I know. I've been giving this a lot of thought. I'm only five points away from passing in cell biology and statistics, and one point away from passing biochem. So all I really need to do for my finals is..."

"Sarah." He interrupted me with a cough and a wave of his hand. "You're talking about getting grades that will allow you to barely pass your courses. Is this what you really want?"

My face became warm.

"I was able to get you through freshman year by rearranging your schedule and mixing in more of the easier classes than we usually do for first-year students." His tone was that of gentle exasperation. "And I figured you could take the harder courses later, when you became better adjusted to the environment here. But, Sarah... This *IS* later."

I felt my mouth and throat get so dry that I was starting to have difficulty swallowing. My body seemed to know where this conversation was heading even if my brain didn't yet.

"You're a sophomore now," he said, "and these classes not only have to be passed, they have to be mastered. It only gets harder from here on out." Dr. Weinstein shifted in his plush swivel chair. He placed his hand over taut lips.

My stomach growled. Not from hunger, but from nerves. It did that every so often, and helped make a difficult time for me just that much more difficult. I pressed my fist firmly against my abdomen in a futile effort to keep all volatile, gurgling acids where they belonged.

He cleared his throat, and let out a heavy sigh. He lifted a pile of papers off his desk, glanced briefly at it, and carelessly threw it back down. "I wish I'd kept a closer check on you, Sarah."

I unfolded the jumbled mess of papers in my lap. I kept my head bent down while he let out another heavy, frustrated sigh and tapped his fingertips on the surface of his desk. A few more seconds of degrading silence went by, but it might as well have been a few hours. I cast my eyes toward the floor. Mentally, all of me was there, splattered on the linoleum.

"Sarah, I... really don't know what else to say." He looked down at his desk and then thoughtfully at my mutilated chapter.

I stood. I was willing this torture to be over.

It would be at least another few minutes of debasement before my wish was granted.

I walked quietly out of his office. With a quick flip of my wrist, I tossed the manuscript in the wastepaper basket by the secretary's desk. Glancing at the time on my cell phone, I realized that there was no sense in staying any later than I already had. I shot out of the building, flipping posted notices up in the air with a rush of wind furiously whipping behind me.

The train station was a few blocks away. A soft breeze

caressed my face, begging me to still love Boston. But it didn't woo me with its charm as I started toward the "T".

I'd been terminated.

Finished.

Done.

I thought about what I'd just gone through, but the state of shock and disgust I was in wasn't allowing it to fully register. I sat down on a metal and wood rail track bench in a shady shelter that marked the Longwood T stop. There was no one around, and so no one to watch me bury my face in my hands and cry. The tears felt hot against my cheeks as they slid downward and clung to the bottom of my jaw. Warm and salty, they trickled over my upper lip, and I quickly swept the side of my forefinger under my nose. I sniffled, and then forced so much air out of my lungs that I gasped.

I wanted to blame somebody.

I needed to blame somebody.

I physically ached to blame somebody.

But who could I really blame for washing out? For maybe following a path that I probably never should have been on in the first place? My mind darted back to the cell biology lab... the pain, the boredom, and discomfort of counting cells smashed under a coverslip in a hemocytometer, much like the images seen in *The Far Side* except without the humor. I winced as I thought of how often I would catch myself staring up at the analog clock hanging over the doorway, literally watching the hours of my life pass me by. The only times I would feel even the slightest bit of levity were when I was asked to write something, like a lab report. I very much enjoyed writing, and feeling that little jolt of satisfaction that came with my fingers hitting the last few letters on the keyboard and turning hazy, amorphous concepts into something concrete and meaningful.

OK. I didn't just enjoy writing.

I loved it.

But I hadn't been accepted into a B.S. program in the pharmaceutical sciences to do what I loved.

And it showed.

I walked outside the shelter and half-heartedly embraced a cool, evening wind that made the trees lining the train tracks rustle and sway. The sky dimmed slightly, and a little green trolley with bright headlights emerged from the brush in the distance. The train slowed to a halt not far from where I stood, and an elderly woman who had just crossed a wide wooden platform a few feet away climbed carefully into it. I turned my gaze away from the steps of the train's entrance, rubbed my eyes, and flopped back down on the bench behind me. After a minute or two, the train doors folded and, seeming nearly as spent as me, it wearily dragged itself away.

A man wearing a cowboy hat became visible upon its departure. He quietly stood with his hands pressed against his hips on the other side of the wooden platform. He looked at first to be waiting for the arrival of a train going in the opposite direction. Then he limped across the tracks and stood close by to where I was sitting. Too close. He pulled a cigarette pack out of the pocket of his shirt, tapped it loudly against the palm of his hand, and stared at the hilly road running parallel to the tracks.

He cleared his throat. "Aren't there usually more people here this time of day?" he asked in a deep smoker's voice. He lifted his hat, swept his hand through long, sandy brown fringe that hung over his eyes, and turned toward me. His eyebrows raised.

I could only stand to look at him peripherally, as I would the sun. I looked down at my cell phone. "It's seven."

"I didn't ask you for the time." Strands of oily hair again fell into his face. He placed his hat back on top of his head and gave me a wide, greasy smile.

I looked away from him. It was just my day to be branded an idiot, apparently. I wondered if I had mascara stains on my cheeks.

"You're here a little early." He continued to smile.

OK. That spooked me. "Excuse me?" I suddenly wasn't concerned about looking like Alice Cooper anymore. The hat and hair covered his eyes, which for a split second, when I caught a gutsy glance of them, almost made him look familiar to me. But I knew I was in about as right of mind as he apparently was at that moment, and so I didn't pay it another thought.

He let out a guttural laugh. He scratched his chest underneath a t-shirt that revealed a patch of protruding beer belly. "I usually see you here later."

I pretended to search for something in my purse.

"I guess you're a nurse?" he asked.

"Student," I said, my busy hand slowing to a halt and fingering the edge of a slip-in eyeglass case. I could feel the warmth of the blood rushing to my face as my heart began to thump loudly in my chest. It was such an odd sensation, as I was otherwise drained to the point of being listless. Did I really want to be giving this person any information about myself?

"What kind of student?" he asked.

A crappy one. "Science. Drug development." I started mumbling, shrugging, "Research. Sort of. I don't know..."

"Drugs, huh?" He placed a cigarette between his lips. "Research, eh? In what? Cancer or heart disease?" He smiled with the cigarette held firmly between his clenched teeth and carefully slid the cigarette pack back into his shirt pocket.

I looked down at the concrete below my feet and pretended to study swirls of dried pink goo wedged in between some crevices. But it was pointless. This was not the kind of man to pick up on social cues and *shut up.*

"I could've guessed science and research and whatnot by just looking at you." He laughed. "You have this... *aura.*" Then he began laughing uncontrollably. The fit culminated in a loud spewing of phlegm behind a wall of

7

the shelter. He cleared his throat and spit a ball of saliva at his feet. "I want to get to know you."

I looked up at him, and no doubt my face told him what I thought about that prospect. There were a number of deal breakers here, not the least of which was the hawking up of mucus.

He clamped his fingers on a metal bar that jutted out from the top of the shelter. His large stomach poked out from underneath the frayed edges of his shirt, and he swung his body back and forth. He was staring at me with a surprised expression, as if I had just appeared in front of him. I supposed he had been gunning for me to squirm or run, as I was just staring back, looking unimpressed.

I should run, really, I told myself. It was the sane, rational thing to do. If nothing else, I was likely to pick up a drug-resistant strain of TB right there on the platform if I stayed. But I was tired. I was tired of running and quite frankly too tired to be afraid.

I opened my mouth. Nothing came out. I looked around, willing a train to appear, willing someone normal and purposeful to stop the nonsense and free me to continue agonizing over what had happened to me earlier in the day. I wanted to focus on having been kicked in the teeth. I'd just been humiliated. Sized up and brought down. And I'd been a nearly willing partner in it all. Was this how the rest of my day would go? The rest of my life?

It was only getting more surreal. My inner city letch laughed and pulled the cigarette pack out of his shirt pocket again, as if this were his signature Hollywood move.

A group of kids headed toward the hut. They stopped at a nearby street lamp and huddled closely together. They exchanged glances and laughed loudly. And I was jealous.

The man looked away from me and stared at a couple of young girls. He turned back toward me. "Red hair. Soft. Long. You have what I like." He made wave motions with his hands and then, when I was not facing him and aware of what was coming at me, he gently traced his grubby forefinger along the side of my cheek in slow motion.

My glasses slid down the bridge of my nose and I quickly pushed them back up. I lifted a clothing catalog that someone had left behind on the bench. I began flipping through it. Mentally, I conjured the long hot shower I would need to feel clean again.

The man kicked some dirt and pebbles with the tip of his untied sneaker. "You been living here long?"

I shook my head. "I don't really feel like talking." Understatement.

He smiled a broad, confident smile. He repeated himself. "Have you been living here long?"

I cocked my head and drew a deep breath, pretending I was OK with all of this, in control. "No. Have you?"

He laughed and drew hard on his freshly lit cigarette. "Nah." He released the smoke through his nostrils. "This could never be my home."

I heard a rumble in the distance yet couldn't decide from which direction the sound was coming. After looking toward my right and then to my left, I saw that two trolleys going in opposite directions were arriving at the T stop at the same time. I walked quietly past the man and toward the kids who were gathering at the train's entrance.

"I'll get us seats," the man said, taking his place in line in front of me.

I looked away from him. I'd had more than I could handle for one day. Defeated and demoralized as I was, I wasn't the silly putty in this weirdo's hands that he apparently thought I was. *Please piss off. Take a hint, or two, or a thousand, and GO AWAY!!!*

"I said I'll get us seats," he said again, more loudly. He was testing me, banking on my broken girl passivity. I must have seemed too delicious of a treat, because I heard him cough up a tittering little laugh. I was his willing victim. And was that really who I was going to keep being?

One of the kids turned around at the sound of my Beantown stalker's voice and looked curiously at us. The man turned his face abruptly away from me and hustled past the kid. He stepped up onto the train and looked over his shoulder to see if I would follow. When our eyes met, I wanted him to see someone transformed. Someone filled with anger, on the verge of overflowing with rage at him, at Weinstein, at myself, at the world.

It was sort of a quiet explosion that left my lungs. "Screw! You!"

The other train had just closed its doors and was preparing to leave. I frantically fumbled in my purse for change or tokens while running across the tracks to try to catch it. The driver must have seen me coming, for as I approached, the doors flew open again. I tossed an extra quarter into the coin receptacle and swung around a nearby metal pole into an available seat. See, world? I was not a complete loser... even if I was now on the wrong train.

The green trolley sluggishly pulled itself away from the stop and began chugging away from the direction of where I lived. Breathing heavily, I looked hard out the window at the dark, passing landscape. I glanced over at a freckle-faced teenage girl sitting on the other side of the trolley. My glance turned into a stare, and I stared until I could no longer distinguish what was her long, silky blond hair and the upturned tip of her shiny, young nose and what was just a reflection in her window. She became a blur, a fuzzy mass that grew more and more distorted as the water in my eyes raised and my lids lowered. Soon, very soon, she was gone.

I stayed on the train as long as I was allowed to. I used my time to drive as many thoughts as I could completely out of my head. I wanted to see nothing, to hear nothing, to feel nothing. I wanted to be in the midst of a void, a soothing, distancing, dulling state of sheer darkness. I wanted no light, no music, no poetry, no conversation. I wanted to be utterly alone.

I listlessly stepped out onto the platform of the last stop and made my way over to a bench that smelled like stale urine. I started to hold my breath and sit down, when another train arrived at the stop. I slowly climbed up its steps, wasted more of my loose change, and then sat down in an empty seat. I tried to ignore the sensation of wetness from some unknown liquid soaking through the backside of my jeans.

The day's events flashed in rapid succession in my mind, and a wave of nausea came over me, forcing me to close my eyes. I rested the backs of my knuckles against my clammy forehead. Once the train pulled away from the platform, I leaned my head against the shiny cold wall next to me and began to feel some relief. The squeaking of the brakes against the rails grew fainter and the rocking motion of the train caused me to drift off into a light sleep.

The train lurched, jolting me awake, causing me to fall forward and hit my chin on the metal back of an empty seat. I rubbed my aching jaw and looked outside the window for clues as to how far the train had traveled since the time I had fallen asleep. It was passing through a moss-covered stone tunnel that looked vaguely familiar but that said nothing about exactly where I was.

The seats ahead of me were mostly vacant. There were just an elderly man and woman sitting a couple of seats away. I was considering asking them what train stop we were approaching when I felt a tap on my shoulder.

"You missed your stop."

The low, gravelly voice was unmistakable, as was the big oily grin that accompanied it.

"You missed your stop," he whispered in my ear, the sour smell on his breath wafting past my nose. He reached toward my elbow and squeezed it. I flinched and pulled away from him. My heart was racing. Instinct and adrenaline willed my feet to do the same but there was nowhere to run.

The train slowed as it approached a station. The old man stood up and began walking to the central exit of the train, trailing his hand along a piece of upper railing. I quickly stood up and followed closely behind him.

"So do you want to get to know me?" The low gravelly voice and oily grin were inches away from the back of my head.

I whisked around and felt the hair I had parted to one side collapse and hang loosely over the center of my forehead. Usually whenever my hair did that, I felt sexy and catlike. Alluring. A vixen. If there was ever a moment I did not want to feel this way, or even worse, *look* this way, it was now. I quickly parted my hair again.

"I still want to get to know you," he said softly. "I *need* to get to know you." He gently took hold of my arm and tried to draw me closer to him.

I felt a sickly chill race through my body. I writhed out of his grasp and shoved him away from me. I pushed against the elderly man's back with my thumbs and tried to hustle him off the train as best as I could without hurting him.

My stalker stepped off the train shortly after I did. "I didn't mean to scare you." The softness of his voice was cloying.

I wasn't sure why, but I stopped walking and looked back at him, curious to see what he would do next. He passed under the diffuse orange glow of a couple of streetlights and leapt onto a wide, wooden platform overlaying the tracks. He dug his hands inside the pockets of his jeans, and staggered away.

I crossed my arms and pressed them tightly against my chest. My eyes followed him until he was completely out of sight. But even then, I wondered, *is he really gone?*

* * * *

I lay awake that night in bed, unblinking, wide-eyed. I curled my toes under a tiny afghan and fought for some warmth while gyrating over hills and valleys in the mattress.

"Sarah, this is really the academic dean's place to say this. But I want you to know that Dr. Vogel and I have talked. The general consensus is that you'd probably do better... re-evaluating your long-term goals and plans." He placed his fingers on his lips and stared blankly ahead. *"Your grades last year were marginally acceptable. Had you not made it through general chemistry, we would have had grounds to ask you to leave the program then."*

I felt an aching tightness in my neck.

He drew a deep breath and slowly let the air out of his lungs. "I wish you the best with whatever you decide to do. You can discuss this with Dr. Vogel, but I'm pretty sure he'll tell you the same thing."

I had to leave. I knew I had to leave. For quite some time I'd known, and yet I still stayed. I had stayed just to tread water and finally drown. *Even hippos can swim,* I thought perversely. And on this night that I lay awake thinking about all of the wrong choices I had made, everything had come together in such a way as to practically escort me away.

I have to leave, I thought, mouthing the words but saying nothing out loud. I dug the pointy nail of my index finger into the lifeline of my palm. *I shouldn't run and hide. I shouldn't, but...* I wondered if I could start fresh by going home, by going back to the place where I never really had the chance to start at all. Home was the hardest place to teach myself to stop being a victim. But it was also likely the most important place to do it.

So I'll go, I thought, the disappointingly elusive sense of courage starting to leak away. It was all too easy to picture myself sitting in a corner of my little Boston loft, not eating, not sleeping, not drinking, not bathing. I would sit there until rigor mortis set in and I'd have to be physically removed and either buried in a local cemetery or propped up at the main gate entrance of one as a gargoyle.

But instead I stood up, brushed my teeth like the good girl I've always been, and flopped back onto my bed to think about which would be the first of the suitcases I would pack. *You ARE going, kid.* I repeated my mantra out loud. "You are going."

Through the floral, transparent curtains of my bedroom window, I watched shadows of tree branches quivering in the moonlight. On the other side of a set of heavy black bars, the window pane was partly lifted up, allowing me to hear the sound of soft breezes flying through the trees. The hypnotic scent of the evening air crept its way through the window screen. I felt myself just starting to relax a little.

Something hard hit the screen. I envisioned a night-blind bird or a sonar-impaired bat slamming into the side of the building and falling unconscious to the ground. I got up and looked out the window, almost wanting to see the stranger standing under a tree in the perfectly mowed grass, looking up at me with his slick grin. I could flip him off. There was a self-tormenting part of me that craved for the nightmare to continue, as if too much of a bad thing would overwhelm me and just leave me numb.

All I saw, though, was the trunk of a tall birch and the dark, shadowy ground beneath it. When I turned back around and looked toward my bed, for a second I saw what looked like the silhouette of a person lying down. I stopped short and felt my knees weaken. I blinked my eyes and the image disappeared.

I lay back down again in my bed, pulled the afghan to my chin, and tried to shut my eyes. I had come to Boston half-crazy, and this latest stint almost finished the job.

You are going.

Chapter 2

It was beyond odd returning to Palenville, New York. It was just a dot in the Catskill Mountains quietly snoozing at the base of Kaaterskill Clove with a resident population barely scraping a thousand. Any bond I may have had at one time with the little hamlet had disappeared long ago, carted away in a strong dusty wind, unassuming off the cemetery grounds and mausoleums. I had no living relatives. If it weren't for my friend, Scott, I would be completely alone.

Swirls of dust danced around me in my new apartment. I pried a sticky window open and watched Scott unload my belongings from his father's pickup truck. It had been around a year and a half since I last saw him, and I was surprised at how much he had changed. No longer plump, his body had become long and lean. His once baby face now had hollowed cheeks covered with dark stubble. Life had aged him in just the short time we had been apart.

He raised a bulky clothing-filled trash bag off the floor while I started unwrapping newspaper-covered glasses. He tied his long, curly dark brown hair back with a rubber band and placed the trash bag down over the threshold of a closet. He peered inside the bathroom, with a toilet and shower just inches apart. "This is perfect, if you're a guy," he said. "If you're running late, you can wash and pee at the same time. Just watch your step when you're done showering." He walked over to the kitchen sink, bordered by a small stove, refrigerator, and wooden cabinets. He filled a paper cup with tap water and guzzled it down quickly, and then pulled a bandana out of his back pocket to wipe the sweat off of his face.

"Scott, you're my freaking landlord," I shot back. "Shouldn't you be selling me on this place?"

He paused. "Oh, yeah. I kind of am, aren't I?"

"I needed a place I could afford," I said.

He lifted two heavy cardboard boxes filled with dishes onto the kitchenette counter. "This box in front of me is probably in the same price range," he said. "Can't think what possessed my parents to invest in this place."

I walked over to a set of French doors that overlooked the front porch. The doors were covered with wooden blinds that blocked out the brown, sun-dried front lawn. I never liked this part of town. "Is this place safe?" I asked, peering through the cracks of the blinds. I gave the doors a shake and asked, "Will these keep anybody out?"

"Everyone knows that nobody has any money out here," he said. "Criminals don't even bother, Sarah."

"It's just that I never had a place so... open like this. How many doors does one place need? Especially a small place like this?"

"Please. Don't deprive this apartment of the only charm it has," he said. "Keep these locked and just use the side entrance." He lifted the wooden blinds up and said, "There's another apartment next door that's the mirror image of this one."

"Do your parents own that, too?"

"No, they don't. But I know no one's living there now," he assured me. "So you've got the whole porch- and yard- to yourself."

I placed a large aquarium tank filled with two golden hamsters on a cedar trunk. "I'll take you to lunch, Scott. I just have to get these guys settled first." I removed the water feeder and replenished it with water from the kitchenette sink.

"Aw, how cute. Sarah and her hamsters. Holy smokes, they're *huge*," he said, leaning over the tank and staring into it. "Hamsters are not supposed to be the size of guinea pigs. Or are they? Do you have your species mixed up here?"

I smiled and shook my head. "They're not that big." I loosely sprinkled dried corn and seeds into a couple of feeding bowls and watched the animals migrate across the tank toward the food.

"Are you feeding them lard?" He observed one of the hamsters as it lowered its little bald head in rolls of fat that cascaded like steps down both sides of its body. "I see the hamster wheel in there. Bet that'll keep you awake at night. I'd tell you to stick them in the bathroom, but I don't think the tank will fit in there." He laughed. "I'm sure they'll get along well with the veteran rats and mice in the ceiling and wall cracks."

"On that note," I said, smiling. "Let's go get something to eat."

* * * *

We stopped off at the requisite local diner with its iconic silver exterior and a bright neon restaurant sign. The whooshing sounds of speeding highway vehicles could be heard a half a mile away from a nearby exit ramp.

"Take this place away and you take away employment for half the people we went to high school with," Scott said. He buffed the hood of the truck with his sleeve. "Take a look," he said, pointing to a "help wanted" sign on a window by the front door. "A true position of envy, serving parsley-studded cholesterol to a bunch of two hundred and fifty pound bikers in mid-life crisis."

We walked inside, and my stomach instantly knotted. I recognized Pamela behind a retro chrome counter pouring an old batch of coffee into a fresh, steaming pot. What used to be long, flowing light blond hair was now short and wispy. Her skin was sallow, her face slightly gaunt. Small crevices cradled her large, blue eyes. She approached us with a concentrated, determined look.

"Hi," I said, softly.

She smiled a sweet, but sad, smile, and handed me a menu. She looked at Scott, laughed, and teasingly hit him on the head with his menu. "Hi, honey!"

"You guys... haven't seen each other since when?" He pointed to both of us.

She looked at me. Still smiling, she shook her head. "I don't know." She started hitting her pen against the little note pad she was about to take orders with. "How you been?" she asked me.

"Do you remember her name?" Scott asked.

"Stop," I mumbled.

Pamela's smile faded. A strained look took its place. "Honestly, I don't remember you spending too much time with all of us neighborhood kids." She narrowed her eyes and turned to Scott. "Sheesh, Scottie! Stop making trouble!" I noticed she was avoiding saying my name.

He snickered. "You guys are so old."

"I'm nineteen, dimwit," Pamela said to him. "You're not even a full year younger than me."

He lifted his chin up toward her and smiled. "I'll have a cheeseburger with onion rings. And a root beer."

She scribbled his order down. She looked at me with a wrinkled brow. A wrinkled but perfectly sculpted brow.

"Tuna on white," I said.

"Drink?" she asked.

"Water."

"With ice," Scott said. "Adds flavor."

Pamela sauntered into the kitchen. I watched her walk a few seconds later to the cash register. She posed by a stack of menus with her hand pressed against the back of her neck.

Should I? I thought.

Her eyes seemed to be fixed on the afternoon sun, its brightness dulled by a clump of cumulus clouds. She looked like a pasty mannequin in a department store. The calm of her skin-deep beauty always had the power to mask whatever was going on underneath it. If there was, in fact, anything really going on.

Closure, I thought. *How sweet the scent. How vibrant the color. How soft and smooth the texture.* It was a lovely flower waiting to be picked, a chance for me at long last to start to bloom. Maybe.

"I'll be back," I said to Scott. I took a deep breath. *Do I really want to do this?*

Pamela stopped posing. She shot a defensive glance at me as I approached her.

"Can I have a work application?" I asked.

She looked at me vacantly, and then stretched her neck to peer through the windows of the kitchen doors as though she were looking for someone. "I wonder if Matt's around," she mumbled, before dutifully reaching behind the register. She pulled out a stapled pamphlet.

I forced a smile and took it from her. Her eyes met mine for a second or two, and then quickly fell to the cash register. She silently sorted out a remaining stack of blank applications and made their edges flush.

When I returned to the table, I found Scott studying tiny indentations in his thumb a fork he was playing with had left. He picked up the pepper shaker, turned it upside down, and attempted to balance it.

"Seriously?" he asked, eyeing the application. "You're kidding, right?"

I shook my head. "Not kidding. Why would you think I was kidding?"

"*Here?*"

"Yes, here," I said.

He pinched the top of the page of the application with his thumb and forefinger and lowered it to the table. "Can I ask you something?"

"What?"

"Are you ever planning on..." He nodded his head at me and made circular motions with his hands suggesting that he wanted me to verbally finish what he started, as though that would make the subject less distasteful for me to talk about. "You know..."

"No," I said. "I'm not planning on going back to school."

"But it was like... over a year of your life..." he said. "That's time you'll never be able to recoup."

My throat tightened and water filled my eyes. "It wasn't where I was supposed to be." I lifted a napkin up out of the dispenser and wiped the tears sliding down the sides of my face. I blew my nose hard and held the napkin under my nostrils. I looked in Pamela's direction to make sure she didn't see me crying. Fortunately, her back was turned.

"She can't see you," Scott whispered.

I made a fist and hit my knee under the table. "I shouldn't have been there," I said. "Going for a degree in science wasn't just hard. It was pointless. I wasn't interested in it. I'm still not interested."

Scott picked up a spoon. He pushed down on its edge with his pinky. "Well, I personally have no interest in 'biology' other than the narco-euphoric effects of prescription pain-killers on the human nervous system... meaning *my* nervous system."

I tried to conjure up a smile, but it was difficult.

"So... what about switching majors?" he asked.

I shook my head. "I'm finished with school," I said. My eyes slipped to the doors of the kitchen, which were swinging back and forth. I then stared at Scott with such intensity that my eyes started to hurt. "I'd hate to think that life is over at 19," I said. "But that's the way it feels."

He shrugged. "Your life is just starting. The only thing that can kill it is the ultimate weapon of destruction... your *mind*." He looked up at me. "Come on, Sarah. You're a smart girl. Switch gears and do something else. Your parents left you money... Invest it in better stock this time around."

Dust yourself off and move on, I thought, finishing the sentiment. I stared at the spoon Scott was playing with. I envisioned the spoon as being my budding career in the health sciences, being more or less mindlessly tinkered with and leading to nothing in particular except a way to pass the time. It was bachelor's or bust. And I went bust. I looked down at my arms just then, and my eyes lowered to my legs. Despite how amputated I may have felt, they were still there. Perhaps what I needed to do now was lower the bar. And the next thing I needed to do was to keep moving. Focus on survival first, success later.

I remembered a sermon I heard as a kid, from one of the wiser people I'd ever known, Pastor Paul. While other kids my age were playing Jacob's Ladder and Cat's Cradle with string or studying the freshly exposed contents of the inner walls of their nostrils on their forefingers, I was actually listening to the man. He was telling us that we had to have faith in whatever plan God had in mind for us. Even if the plan was different from our own, even if we didn't like it. We just had to believe that God knew what was best for us, and follow along.

The meaning behind the words didn't penetrate too deeply back then, probably because life was only just budding at the time, with no real "plans" to speak of, and I was too young to find much relevance. But I nonetheless still remembered what he had said.

"So what about you?" I asked. I needed to shift the focus.

"What *about* me?" he asked back.

"What are you planning on doing?"

"What do you mean... *planning* on doing?"

"You know what I mean."

"No," he said, shaking his head and chuckling. "I don't. What makes you think I'm planning on doing anything other than what I'm doing right now?"

"What exactly is it that you are doing?"

"Living," he said, defensively. "Is there a problem with that?"

I lowered my eyes to the table. "Why do you feel like you can't talk to me?"

He wrinkled his forehead. He moaned. "I can talk to you. For heaven's sake, I talk to you all the time."

"You talk to me... about me," I said. "You don't talk about yourself."

"So what do you want me to do?" he asked.

"*Talk.*"

"Talk about what?" He glanced quickly into my eyes and then stared down at the table. He turned around abruptly and stared at the swinging doors of the kitchen.

"So you're trying to get me to go back to school, but you're not considering it for yourself?"

"I need money for that," he said. "You have money. I don't."

"Your parents won't help you?" I asked.

"They're giving me free room and board," he said. "The buck stops there as far as they're concerned."

"There's financial aid."

"I know," he said, starting to sound irritated. "I know everything that you know, OK? I'm not as unworldly as you think."

"I never said you were." I shifted in my seat and clenched my fists tightly underneath the table. Focusing on Scott instead of myself was for whatever reason not making me any less tense. Maybe it didn't matter who we were talking about. Life aspirations was just an uptight subject, overall. There was no dodging it.

He impatiently turned toward the kitchen. "I can't think of anything that I really want to do with my life that college or any kind of higher education could prepare me for," he said. "To me, the biggest frauds in the world are the ones who puke up candy-coated Shakespeare and Poe, hand it to you on an expensive pewter dish, and tell you that if you eat all of it up and don't leave anything behind, you can have a job for dessert... four costly years later. Not only is it impossible to get a decent job *with* a college degree, but you also come out of it tens of thousands of dollars in debt. And you're completely, hopelessly unprepared to survive in a world that's nothing like the padded duck and pigeon decorated playpen you spent the most critical four years of your life in. You come out of your little collegiate fantasy land a naive mass of fodder getting worked to the bone and brainwashed into believing that someone did you some kind of *favor* by hiring untalented, loser wastes like you in the first place." He paused. "Not interested. Nope. Not for me."

I laid a napkin across my lap and took a deep breath, exhaling very slowly. "So nothing interests you?"

"I have one interest," he said, staring deeply into my eyes.

"What's that?"

"Fleeing the confines of the mundane," he said. "Look, I'm fine, Sarah." He pinched his stubbly chin. "I'm actually more than fine."

"More than fine?" I asked. "How's that?"

"Unlike average sheeple..." he said, "I mean unlike average working men, I'm not falling prey to all the evil that's out there."

"*Evil*?" I asked.

"The evil deeds," he whispered, "of the Illuminati." A tray of food appeared near Scott's cheek. Pamela gently placed his cheeseburger and onion rings in front of him and gave him a smile. His root beer followed.

"The Illuminati, Scott? You're a conspiracy theorist?" I tried to focus on our conversation but couldn't help but be distracted by Pamela's spindly arm crossing in front of me to place my tuna sandwich down on the table. I looked up at her, stupidly and longingly awaiting a smile as well.

I got nothing.

"Did you know that there's this small elitist group that controls and manipulates the government and media?" Scott started cramming onion rings into his mouth. "They do it through central banking, and they purposefully cause inflation, war, and depressions. We're talking the owners of private banks in the Federal Reserve System, leaders in the energy cartel, lead government officials..."

I stared at him blankly.

"They want to control everything... It's the New World Order. A one world government and currency. Land and property and... people," he said. "Well, they can't control me as long as I am who I am... or am not... and as long as I continue to do what I do... or don't do." He separated the breading from an onion ring and ate the breading by itself. "Less is more in today's world, Sarah."

I remained quiet. But secretly, I liked what he was getting at. *Think big, live small.*

"If I do nothing, or next to nothing, I do it for the good of mankind. It's the ultimate of altruism, and the world should thank me." A piece of chewed breading flew out of his mouth and landed in a narrow vase of wilted flowers. He stuck his finger in the hole of an onion ring and made it dance around his fingertip.

Two pasty white arms crept over his shoulders and rested lightly against his chest. I looked above his head to see Pamela beaming seductively down at him.

"Enjoying the food?" she breathed into his hair.

"As much as always," he sang. He shoved an onion ring into his mouth and raised his eyebrows at her. She kept one arm around him and stepped to his side. She pressed her bosom against his cheek. "Scotty's our best customer," she said. She glanced quickly at me and looked adoringly down at him. "It's amazing with what you eat that you can stay so thin."

He shrugged. "I fantasize a lot. Burns calories." He slipped his arm around her waist.

"You fantasize, huh?" She smiled.

"Just me," he whispered into her shoulder. "And you, undressing in your bedroom, a tree branch, and my binoculars."

"Keep it up," she said, giggling and pushing him away. "I'll have to punish you." She sauntered toward new customers that had walked through the front door.

I sat quietly, and watched Scott watching Pamela.

"Eat," Scott said, suddenly. He noticed that I was picking at my sandwich.

"I am," I mumbled. I lifted a piece of bread crust up to my lips.

"You all right?" Scott asked. He picked a few crumbs off of his plate with the tip of his forefinger and placed them in his mouth.

I looked down at my mostly uneaten sandwich. "Uh-huh." It occurred to me then that I was starving. But not really for food.

Chapter 3

I sat on the dusty floor of my apartment and unloaded textbooks from a cardboard box. For some reason I brought them with me, though there was little chance I would ever look through them. Just the sight of their faded covers was making my stomach braid itself.

I lifted a thin manila folder and opened it. It was filled with a dozen or so sheets of lined loose leaf paper that had smudgy prose scribbled in different places from my junior high school days. I pulled one of my old poems out and read it quietly to myself. It was depressing and morbid, like most of what I'd written back then.

I turned around to look at Scott. He was lying lifelessly on my bed. His arms were tightly pressed against his body, and he was staring at the screen saver on my computer. He belched loudly, and then pretended to catch the noxious gas in the air and blow it in my direction.

"No date on a Friday night?" I asked. "All that charm wasted?"

"It's enough for me to know that they all want me." He rolled over onto his side and squeezed his long, muscular legs together. "And none of them can have me."

"Why is that?"

He paused and scratched the back of his thigh. "Because I know the reality can't possibly live up to the fantasy... on their end or on mine. I'd like to delay the inevitability of mutual disappointment for as long as I'm able to. I know at some point I'll have to come in for a landing. But for now, I'm just going to enjoy the flight. Do you have any unsalted peanuts?"

I shook my head.

"Salted peanuts?" he asked.

I shook my head again. "Your whole life is going to be over by the time you realize that you've been dreaming it away."

He laughed. "Look who's talking."

"I'm not sure I have any dreams," I said.

"Or peanuts." He stared up at the ceiling and squinted his eyes. "You have dreams," he said.

"Yeah? How do you know that?"

"I know because I've seen the passionate side of you. It may have been a while ago since you last showed it, but I know it's there. And a passionate person can't live without dreams."

I knew he was referring to Gary, without naming names. "What if the passion gets sucked out of you?" I asked, also referring to Gary, without naming names.

"It can't," he said. "It's as much a part of you as your heart is. You can't live without a heart. You can't live without passion. It might get cooled from time to time, but it's always there. Just waiting to be reheated. Waiting to be revived. Waiting to chase after dreams."

It is the summertime, just a couple of months away from the start of my freshman year in college. I step over the pebbles, twigs, and fallen tree branches that lead to Angel Rock Leap, a shallow ravine dotted with mossy stones and pointy rocks and guarded by sugar maples, birches, and alders. A nearby forty foot precipice casts an ominous shadow over Kaaterskill Creek's gurgling waters, a gray catbird circling its apex. As I near the watering hole, the sight of Gary sitting on a flattened stone becomes clearer. He is wearing jeans and a t-shirt, which surprises me since we have always met here to go swimming.

"Gary!" I yell.

He does not respond.

Assuming he cannot hear me, I continue tiptoeing around poison ivy, fighting off mosquitoes, and moving closer to the water and rocks. The moon can just be seen in the sky. A brisk evening breeze has begun to set in.

"Gary, didn't you hear me calling you?"

He still does not respond.

"Is there anything wrong?"

He shrugs. Finally, he turns to look at me. "You're wearing a bathing suit? I mentioned on the phone that I just wanted to talk."

I am suddenly feeling underdressed. I nervously pull out a set of cut-off jean shorts from my satchel and throw a towel around my shoulders. "What's wrong?"

He places his hand over his mouth and blows forcefully through his fingertips. He reaches into his shirt pocket and pulls out a soft pack of menthol cigarettes. I watch him light one, never remembering him smoking before. He draws the choking fumes deep into his lungs and watches as steady streams of smoke flow outward through his nostrils. He sighs and says, "You probably can guess that I'm not in the best of moods right now."

"What's going on?" I am standing.

He laughs loudly. "Could you just throw me in?" He lies down on the rock and stares up at the pale yellow haze of the moon. He flicks his ashes over the rock's edge into the water, which is now turning black like the sky. "I hate my life!" he yells with anger, his voice echoing off the cliffs in the distance.

I shiver under my towel and reach out to stroke his hair. He slaps my hand away. "Don't touch me!" Then he says in a low, strained voice, "Please..."

"What is wrong with you?"

"So much more than you can handle." He slowly sits up on the rock and throws his cigarette into the water. "Ask me if I'm in love with you."

I am silent.

"Go ahead. Can you ask me?"

I open my mouth, but no words come out.

"You can't ask me, and I can't tell you," he says, staring down at his floating cigarette.

My stomach is aching. I find I have to sit down on the rock. I wrap my arms around my bent legs and rest my chin on my knees. I stare at the reflection of the moon in the water.

"I'm sorry," he offers. "I've got to be honest with you."

"Is it someone else?" I am still staring down into the water.

He shakes his head. "There's no one I want to be with. The only thing I want is to be alone."

"I don't," I say. I am blinking my eyes. They are starting to sting. So he wanted to meet just to say he wanted to be alone.

"I can't help you," he says.

I lower my head in my folded arms.

"I really need to be by myself." He abruptly stands up, turns in the direction of the woods and walks away. He leaves me only with crickets chirping underneath a full moon.

I lifted up an introductory statistics book and quietly began thumbing through the pages. Even though I couldn't see anything, I kept my eyes fixed on the blur of page corners. "I'm afraid to waste more time on anything that might not go anywhere," I murmured.

Scott sat up. "Sarah..."

"What?"

"You're living in the past." He laid back down and put his hands over his face. He shook his head back and forth on my pillow. "Do you realize that your life comes to a grinding halt every time something doesn't go the way you wanted it to?" He continued to roll around on my bed with his eyes covered.

I made a funny noise with my mouth. But I knew he was right. I wouldn't have been there in person for him to say this to if I didn't secretly agree with him. I had come back to Palenville for a reason. Didn't I? Was it to be a victim again or to plot some sort of post-victim life?

Scott grabbed a bottle of seltzer off of the floor by the bed and guzzled it down. He loudly screwed the metal cap of the bottle back in place and sat, looking at me.

I sat quietly with my shoulders slumped forward.

"What is it?" he asked.

I sighed.

"Overdraft protection for your thoughts." He wiggled his eyebrows as if begging me to notice how clever he was.

I rubbed my eyes with my fingertips. I turned to face him. "Maybe it wouldn't hurt talking about it. I guess."

"Are you sure you want to?"

"No."

"Well, then... I'd better seize this opportunity before you change your mind." he said.

I sighed again. "Forget it. It's stupid. It doesn't matter."

Scott leaned toward me, put both of his hands on my shoulders and stared deeply into my eyes. "If you don't tell me, I promise I will erupt into a gaseous explosion so intense it will very closely resemble a nuclear meltdown."

"I don't feel like talking anymore," I said, shaking free from his grip.

After waiting a moment for a response from me yet not receiving one, he whined, "Sarah..." He was annoying in the way a puppy might be.

"Being back here... I don't know how to explain it. Seeing people like..." I paused. "All the doubts I ever had about myself... All the reasons this town gave me to doubt myself still seem to be there. This goes back as far as junior high. Well... actually further than that even." I pinched the corner of my lower lip and stared down at my feet. "I was hoping that these feelings would be gone, so I could start over again. I could come home, but not really. It wouldn't be home as I once knew it, and I wouldn't be the person in doubt this town once knew."

There was silence. Scott cupped my chin in his hand, squeezing my cheeks so that my lips were puckered. He smiled agreeably when he got the effect he wanted. "Why must you dwell on such ridiculous things?" he asked.

"I knew you wouldn't understand."

"No, I don't understand. So much time has gone by. Who remembers? And who cares?"

"I guess I do," I said.

He stood up. He paced the floor with his hands clasped behind his back.

I lay down on the bed and rested my arm across my eyes to block the shine coming from an uncovered fluorescent light bulb in the ceiling.

He pointed toward the French doors and said, "You know, there are hordes of people out there with problems that go way beyond the small confines of their imaginations. There are people who *wish* their personal tragedies were years behind them."

"I know," I said. "I have to clear my plate because there are people starving in Africa."

Scott stood still, scratching the back of his head. He grimaced. "If I were you, I'd be more concerned about finding a job than worrying about what some walking and talking congenital defect, some unfortunate product of a prophylactic gone awry, said to you five or six years ago."

"I have a job."

"You do?"

"I start at the diner on Sunday."

Scott hung his head low. He slowly raised his eyes. "You're still set on taking that?"

"Yes," I said. "You know, you're starting to annoy me."

"Sorry," he said, dejectedly.

"You're still living at home and collecting money from your parents' tenants?" I hissed. "Still doing landscaping in the summers? Occasionally during the winter, so long as it isn't snowing too hard or the temperature isn't too cold? Still set on doing that?" I thought about my free-spirited friend and his free-spirited ways. It didn't seem fair for this to only apply to him.

He turned his head and looked toward the side entrance. "I didn't mean to upset you," he sulked.

I sat up on the bed too quickly and made myself dizzy. I slowly lay back down again and gently eased my head into my pillow. "We all do what we feel we need to do, Scott," I said, feeling suddenly less defensive and instead more proud and resolute. "Support me and my choices, and I'll do the same for you."

He gazed at me with wide, pleading eyes. "Really, Sarah. I'm sorry," he said. "And if you don't forgive me, I'll erupt into a gaseous explosion..."

"Flatulence will get you nowhere."

"I beg to differ," he said. "I've got proof."

I smiled at him. "Get out of here."

He stared at me for a few seconds. He moved silently toward the doorway. "Good to have you back, Sarah." He opened the door and shut it quickly behind him.

Chapter 4

Sunday arrived with gray skies and air heavy with moisture. I quietly stood on my front lawn, taking deep breaths. The sandy concrete of the street ahead was shaded on both sides by dark, looming willows. A nearby dilapidated white fence was strangled by deep green ivy twisting along its length. The road turned in the far distance up a steep hill and disappeared into a thick assembly of trees. These trees comprised a natural partition that divided the affluent part of town from the hole I was calling home these days.

The thought of huge, stone mansions that I used to see out there as a child came to mind, towering over stretches of rolling fields and rocky, sparkling creeks. I used to feel that so long as I continued walking high up into the mountains, there would always be something new and beautiful waiting to be uncovered. And it was only when darkness fell and my feet ached that I was forced to turn back from what I came to believe was paradise.

I loved exploring. And discovering. I realized how fascinated I was with people, how much I wanted to understand them, and write about them, and write about... life. But I couldn't write about people so long as I held myself back from getting close to them. And I couldn't write about life so long as I held myself back from living it.

I thought about what would have happened had I stayed in college, had I pursued a career in research. Any writing I did would likely have been inspired by what I was doing and with whom. And I supposed the inspiration to put pen to paper would have been the one isolated perk of continuing to spend time doing what I generally didn't like with people I didn't particularly care for.

Like my Ulf Fucher story.

That was a dandy. I'd written it in my second semester in college, a byproduct of the ramblings of Earl, a jaded postdoc mentoring me in one of my rotation labs. Day after day, he described what happens when you take a bunch of nerdy, type A+ socially awkward shut-ins and force them to work in very small quarters with each other for months on end near radioactive material and other toxins. What happens when this small group of scientists goes about their business day after day in painfully close proximity under harsh acne and wrinkle accentuating fluorescent lights and amid the faint smell of sulfur-based compounds.

Earl took a seat toward the back of the conference room near the refreshment table. It had been a long-standing tradition of his at symposiums to find an imposing pot of coffee and heavily layered platter of sliced cantaloupe and salsa chips to hide behind in case he nodded off.

Dr. Ulf Fucher quietly stood behind the podium, peering curiously out at his slowly growing audience from behind the rims of his spectacles. There was a hint of a smile on his smoothly shaven face as he pretended to sort through his notes. Earl knew from experience that this confident smirk meant Ulf was perched and ready to blow all of them out of their undergarments with what would undoubtedly be a stellar display of tightly controlled experimental data, each successive set laying out a more and more solid foundation supporting Ulf's latest earth axis-tilting and world-as-we-once-knew-it revolutionizing hypothesis.

The lights were dimmed. With all of the dramatic build-up of tension in the room as they braced themselves for Ulf's presentation, Earl half-expected to see the cloudy emissions from smoke machines enveloping the podium and projector screen in front of the 150 or so fruit slice and tortilla chip munching spectators.

As Ulf droned on, Earl couldn't help but notice that the graphs and figures flashing on the projector screen behind him looked profoundly similar to graphs and figures that Earl had recently generated and had openly shared with him in what Earl was led to believe was a scientific collaboration. Perhaps the graphs and figures were the same as those Earl had produced on his own, and perhaps, Ulf was going to give Earl an acknowledgement at the end of his talk? Earl moved his body to the edge of his chair and squinted at the contents of the slide being shown.

"The Anti-Proliferative Effects of CTB006 on the V299D Point Mutant." Yes, the title of the slide was perfectly in sync with a set of experiments Earl had done several weeks earlier. But no, the corresponding line

graphs that sat underneath the slide's title were not ones that Earl had generated. They were the result of someone else's work.

"I don't understand this," Earl said, closing the door of his supervisor's office behind him. "Why is Ulf having his techs replicate experiments he knows I've already done?"

"I'm sorry," Dr. Whitfield said.

"He didn't even mention me at the talk. I thought this work was ours. I was the one who found CTB. It was my work that led to the discovery of this drug."

"I know." Dr. Whitfield pushed the center of his glasses with his forefinger and cusped his hands over some papers on his desk. "You found CTB in a screen for inhibitors of V299D. Ulf originally identified the V299D mutation. This is important work, and you've both made tremendous contributions."

"Thank you," Earl said.

"I thought the two of you could work together on this, Earl," Dr. Whitfield said. "I'm under the impression, though, that Ulf wants to work on V299D independently."

Earl felt a sickly warmth surface in his cheeks. His mouth was suddenly saliva-free, as though he had a dentist's question mark-shaped suction device balanced under the base of his tongue. "So... what does this mean for the work I've been doing for the past five months?"

Dr. Whitfield looked down at his clasped fingers, parts of which were beginning to turn white from lack of circulation. "I'd say, Earl, just keep moving along with it. I realize this is a difficult situation."

Earl looked down at the floor and nodded slowly.

Dr. Whitfield straightened his back and leaned away from his desk. "Just give it some more time, OK?"

Earl continued nodding. "OK," he said.

Earl walked outside and tried to lose himself in the comfort of a soft breeze swimming through his hair and tickling his neck. But he was finding it impossible to lose himself in anything other than an onslaught of saddening, worrisome thoughts that bounced off the walls of his brain like a silver sphere in a pinball machine. What kind of life was it, Earl was beginning to wonder, working long hours in a laboratory and getting little money for, more often than not, disappointing results? What kind of life was it, surrounded by colleagues who were likewise working long hours in a laboratory and getting little money for, more often than not, disappointing results? And what kind of life was it, getting results every so often that were anything but disappointing, only to have those results confiscated by overworked, underpaid, and disappointed colleagues?

Ulf was sitting at his desk when Earl arrived at the lab the following day. He glanced up at Earl briefly as he approached, and he grunted something that was barely audible and generally unintelligible. He shuffled some papers around on the surface of his desk until he found one that he could pretend to be engrossed in.

Earl thought about slowing his pace down and confronting him about being a sneaky, conniving thief with no respect or regard for the hard labor and fierce pride of certain coworkers. Coworkers he apparently got a charge out of watching turn into flaky, decaying carcasses after the very essence of their being was sadistically siphoned out and incinerated alongside the lab's weekly build-up of biohazard waste. Yet Earl continued to walk swiftly past him and toward his own desk, where he pretended to be engrossed in his own stacks of meaningless notes and scribbling.

It all reminded Earl of junior high or high school antics, except in this case instead of the mean kids beating up on the nerdy introverts, it was an all-nerd group of adults that was beating up on each other. One would think that all of them would be a bit more gentle and compassionate toward each other, as they all likely went through the same growing pains and small traumas that convinced them something other than charm or good looks would be needed to catapult them to success in life.

He wondered if that was what made them all so intense, so guarded, so serious, and so... mean. These geeks he had to deal with every day were an utter mystery to him, especially in light of the fact that he knew what they all went through. He knew it because it was what HE went through. You'd think they'd all be a whole lot nicer to one another, having finally funneled into a social mecca specially designed to comfortably house the freakiest of the freaky and the nerdiest of the nerdy. But instead they were arrogant, angry, petty, and... well... annoying as all hell.

A wad of whipped cream slipped off a pastry Earl had started eating and landed on his desk. Without thinking, he dipped his pinkie in it, scooped it up, and put it in his mouth. Only after he was in the middle of swallowing it did he remember all of the times he had laid plastic bags filled with dead mice on the desk top, and never washed its surface afterward.

Earl felt a painful throbbing sensation behind both of his temples. He reached for a pen and started to jot down a list of experiments that needed to be done. Yet the peripheral sight of the back of Ulf's bowl-shaped hair made him stop in mid-sentence and toss the pen into a drawer. "What's the point?" Earl mumbled to himself. He lowered his head into his hands and pressed hard against his temples with the tips of his thumbs.

He stood up, walked over to their -20 degree Celsius freezer and angrily pried the door away from a thick layer of frost that had formed on its shelves and walls. His eyes fell on a pale yellow container labeled "CTB." He lifted it, pulled off its cap, and removed an unlabeled vial filled with a fluffy white powder. His eyes slowly drifted over to Ulf. He pushed the unmarked vial into a bank of frost behind some storage boxes toward the back of the freezer. His eyes narrowed and shifted toward Ulf again. Before putting the empty "CTB" canister back into its original place, he dropped a different unmarked vial into it. It was a vial that

*contained a drug prohibited from going onto further
clinical development because of demonstrated rat toxicity.*

*Earl drew a deep breath and quietly closed the freezer
door. Cold vapors of deceit and immorality escaped from
the freezer and swirled around under the lab's bright
fluorescent lights before following him back to his desk.
They began to dissipate once he sat down and stared hard
at the back of Ulf's head, proudly perched between his two
stiff shoulders. They completely disappeared when Ulf
turned his head partly toward Earl, his trademark
mischievous smirk in plain view.*

*Earl knew who Ulf was. But who was Earl? Where did
Earl come from? What brought Earl to this point?*

*He thought back to graduate school, and the many
late nights he spent sprawled out on the surface of an
empty, abandoned desk, too tired to keep standing and yet
so determined to finish a timely experiment that he was
unable to go home. With every failed experiment or
disproved hypothesis came another premature gray hair
and deepening of two creases in his forehead just above the
bridge of his nose. On good days, he would immerse
himself in the lab for hours, perched over a set of plastic
trays holding multi-colored solutions, and reveling over
new insights, and sudden clarity. But then there were the
bad days, when he obstinately struggled in the bowels of
the laboratory, unhappily breathing in its stale air and
squinting under its bright fluorescent lights, only to emerge*

at night knowing less than he knew when he had arrived that morning.

He felt that his life was similar to that of a hardened criminal's, except unlike the hardened criminal who's relieved from his or her suffering in the end, he would be fated to a lifetime of more of the same. He was certain that one day he would wake up to see himself with wild, graying, untamed hair, and crossed eyes hidden behind thick, horn-rimmed spectacles. He'd have a huge fleshy protuberance on his back, and he'd be limping and mumbling obscenities under his breath as he carried a glass beaker of dry ice and ethanol fumes to his young, socially retarded apprentice cowering and quivering behind an empty liquid nitrogen tank.

There was no good reason Earl could think of for why he chose a career in research. The image he had of himself over the years, conversing in strange tongues with his erudite scholarly colleagues outside ivy-covered walls, was shattered when he realized that he had merely become an older and geekier version of what he used to be. He had grown from being a socially-inept, nerdy adolescent to a socially-inept, nerdy adult wondering why he couldn't have tried to be better at sports.

Earl was a pedagogic person in a pedagogic world, bursting at the seams with all the sickening, sacchariferous knowledge that he had been stuffed with for years, forging ahead in the same cosmos that continued to insulate him

49

from a reality he knew was out there, but never gave
himself the opportunity to experience.

Or at least that was my take on it. I had a feeling it
would be Scott's take on it, too, based on some of the
things he was saying while stuffing onion rings into his
mouth at the diner.

It was my take, as long ago as my freshman year, on
the trajectory I was becoming more and more convinced I
should never have been on.

And was right to step off of.

* * * *

Walking across the shadowy pavement to my car, I
stared back at the fog-blanketed porch in front of the
building. The studio apartment next door had been dark and
quiet ever since I moved in. The silence that came with
having the entire first floor of the building to myself was
just starting to change from lonely to endearing. I was
actually looking forward to hearing the pitter-patter of the
hamsters' metal running wheels after I closed my eyes late
at night. I eagerly anticipated the occasional squeaking of
floor boards in the ceiling and muffled scratching noises of
mice inside the walls.

I walked back toward my studio and entered it through
the side door. Once back inside, I walked toward the
French doors and wrestled with the musty lock that held
them together. I lifted the latch and pried the doors apart,
and slowly stepped onto the porch. My two hundred and

fifty dollar a month ensemble of naked wood and rusty nails.

I turned toward the vacant and supposedly mirror image of my studio. I walked over to the set of glass doors that guarded it, trying to see past some loosely hanging blinds on the other side. At first I could only see a small square window with a crack running diagonally across it that looked like it was sitting above a kitchen counter. Just like in my place. The sink in the center of the counter may have been just as small as the one I was still trying to get used to.

Let's see…

I sprung away.

Wait.

I thought I saw someone. But then again, I seemed to be prone to hallucinations as of late.

Nah. Uh. Hmmm.

Maybe?

I hustled back into my apartment and quietly clicked the lock. And I wondered if perhaps Scott was wrong.

* * * *

I spent the first twenty minutes at the diner fishing through waitress uniforms in a cluttered storage room. After finally finding one in a petite size at the very bottom of a cardboard box, I slipped it on and headed into the kitchen.

I stood near the owner and waited for him to finish a conversation with one of the cooks. Beads of sweat clung to his scarlet cheeks and forehead. As he talked, he swept a handkerchief across his hot skin to absorb the droplets that reappeared after every swipe. He caught a glimpse of me in his periphery. He pulled a stack of menus out from underneath his armpit and handed them to me.

"Hi, Sarah. Give these to new customers and walk them to an empty table," he said, mechanically. He then resumed his conversation.

I walked to the cash register and stood near it for a while. I stared mindlessly out the front door. Money for mindlessness.

"So, they've got you hostessing," Pamela said, circling around me like a vulture. She loudly snapped a piece of chewing gum. "We're short on waitressing staff. Why do they have you doing this?"

"I guess just to get me started," I said, surprised by the sound of her voice even though I knew I would see her. I had actually been hoping to see her. "I don't have any experience in waitressing."

"You don't need experience!" she said, cackling. "You just need to know how to move faster than a shooting star." She pulled the chewed piece of gum from her mouth and placed it in an ashtray on a nearby table. "I hate it here."

"You do?" I felt a sudden rush of warmth. She was sharing something with me.

She nodded.

"Have you always worked here? I mean, since we graduated?" I wanted her to share more.

She turned away from me for a moment and looked nervously toward the swinging doors of the kitchen. Then she turned to face me again. "I just want to make sure Matt isn't standing by the windows there waiting to pounce," she whispered.

"Oh," I said. Her breath smelled like strawberries.

She popped a fresh piece of chewing gum into her mouth. "No, I haven't always worked here. I went to college but ended up leaving."

"Oh," I said. I nodded sympathetically.

"Don't hold a benefit for me," she said. "I'd say I've done more in the last couple of years than most people have done in their entire lives."

"Really?"

"Yeah, really," she said. Her blond, shapely eyebrows hung low in her forehead and her eyes were serious and penetrating. "You name it, I did it."

"Like what?" I asked.

"Like what..." she breathed. "Like acting. I dabbled in acting. I did a little modeling. A little dancing..."

"Uh-huh."

She pushed her tongue against the back of her front teeth and exposed the wad of gum in her mouth. "Then one stupid thing led to another, and I wound up here," she said. She stared past me and tousled her short, wispy locks.

"Pamela!" Matt yelled from the back of the diner.

"I'm working!" she yelled back. She picked a dishcloth up from a table and started to wipe it down.

"Heading out!" Matt yelled again. "Be back in a half hour! Maybe an hour! Give Sarah help if she needs it!"

"OK!"

The kitchen doors swung back and forth and Matt disappeared. Pamela clasped her hands together and said, cheerfully, "We have an hour to do nothing. Sundays are so slow here." She sat down at the table she had cleaned off and motioned for me to join her. She smiled wryly and asked, "Why are you here?"

It is ninth grade home economics class. Groups of us are seated at rectangular activity tables. I am placed at the same table as Pamela and her clique of friends, each seated with their elbows carelessly resting on its laminate surface. She is glaring at me as I begin to fumble with the pattern of a skirt I am assigned to make.

"Why are you here?" she asks me. She manages to convey an awful lot with those words. My very existence irks her.

I look up.

"Why don't you sit over there?" she says loudly, pointing toward an eclectic group of lonely-looking girls sitting together at another table. "They're more your style."

"Yeah," adds a small-framed Malaysian girl sitting next to her.

"We don't want you here," Pamela continues.

I stare down at my blueprint and begin to tear at its edges.

"Go over there," she says, rising up out of her seat.

I flatten the pattern out in front of myself and lean my head over it to study its details. Pamela walks over to me, lifts the blueprint up off of the table, and quickly tears it into small pieces.

"Get over there," she says.

The teacher stands up from behind her desk and asks, "Is everything all right?"

"Miss Gould?" Pamela says, running over to her desk. "Is the seating arrangement you gave us final, or can we sit wherever we want?"

"You can move around if you need to," the teacher says.

"Good," Pamela says with a smile. She returns to our table and pulls my chair out from underneath me. I lose my balance, but grip the table hard and keep myself from falling. I collect the torn remains of my blueprint and quietly join the lonely-looking girls at their table.

The sun emerged from behind a cloud and shined brightly through the large, open window of the diner. Its warmth and intensity drew me back to the present.

"You OK?" Pamela asked me. She reached across the table and tapped my arm.

I looked blankly at her.

"You look deep in thought."

"No," I said. "I'm not thinking about anything." I crossed my legs under the table. My foot knocked into her knee and caused her to jump in her seat. "Sorry."

"That's all right," she said. She rubbed her bony kneecap. "I was asking you why you came here."

"Here, the diner? Or here, Palenville?"

"I mean, where were you living before?" she asked.

"Boston."

"Boston... Wow. That's a beautiful city. You're *crazy* for leaving."

"Yeah," I shrugged. "I don't know..."

"There's got to be something missing up in your head for you to come all the way back here from there," she said. She picked up a straw wrapper and twisted it with her long, thin fingers. "What made you leave?"

I closed my eyes. *One stupid thing led to another...* I thought. "I was in a program. For pharmaceutical sciences. I was going for a bachelor's."

Pamela eyed me suspiciously. "Pharmaceutical sciences?" she repeated. "Sounds impressive."

I nodded. I had the sense that I might have been handing her ammo.

"Well then what are you doing waitressing?"

I was quiet. The pin was out of the grenade.

"Did you flunk out?" she asked with a knowing smile.

I had boxed myself into a corner. My *stupid, moronic* honesty had fenced me in. When would I ever learn? I slowly nodded. Ka-BOOM!

"That's too bad," she said. Her mouth twisted to give her a concerned look. "There's nothing worse than a dream that never comes true." Something told me that unless Pamela's lifelong dream was to be a waitress in a truck stop diner, she could probably tell me a thing or two about the elusiveness of dreams.

She squinted her eyes as if she was straining to remember something. "You used to hang out with Denise Something, right? Or Debbie?"

I am eating lunch with Dawn in the junior high school cafeteria. Boys from the football team are sitting at a nearby table with Pamela and her girlfriends, pointing at us and giggling as they aim grape seeds in our direction.

Dawn and I stare down at our food. We try to ward off the assaults with our hands. Dawn loses her temper and yells, "Knock it off already!"

"Hey, look! One of the hutch midgets is talking!" A football player throws a full, juicy green grape at Dawn and hits her in the head. She sits back down. Her face is red.

Pamela stands up and struts toward a large garbage pail. She is carrying her cafeteria tray. On her way, she passes by our table and tilts her tray so that a small pile of grape pits slides off and falls onto our table.

"Oops... Sorry," she says. She places her fingers on her lips and giggles. "I've always had such bad aim." She turns around to her friends and smiles. She pours a full

carton of milk over the surface of our table. She stands for a moment, watching the white, slurry mass glide off the edges of the table and carry floating grape seeds to the floor. Then she hits the top of Dawn's head with the palm of her hand. "You're disgusting," she says. "Clean this up." She turns her back to us and briskly walks away.

"Sarah?" Pamela waved her hand in front of my face. "What's with you? Did you get enough sleep last night?"

I moved my head around as if to gyrate my brain back. I looked around the nearly empty diner. "Not really."

"Insomnia?" she asked.

I shrugged. I found myself not wanting to talk. I found myself not wanting *her* to talk. The closure I had been pining away for was looking more and more like an endless, seamless gaping black hole that in many ways resembled this chick's mouth.

A group of boys wearing trendy backwards baseball caps burst through the door. They wavered near the entrance. I handed them menus and led them to a large table in the center of the diner.

"What kinds of clubs did you belong to in high school?" Pamela asked when I returned to our table.

"Me?"

She laughed. "Who else would I be talking to?"

I smiled weakly. *Your mama,* I thought. "Poetry club."

She was quiet for a moment, as if she were waiting for more. "Was that it?"

"I was a member in the eleventh *and* twelfth grades," I said, realizing as I was saying it that I was highlighting my geekiness and loserdom two-fold.

She smiled and cocked her head, and wasted no time. "I was in... photography... twirling... cheerleading... gymnastics... track..."

"We're ready to order," one of the boys called out, interrupting her. His forefinger was sticking up in the air.

She glanced over toward him. Her eyes fell for a moment to the floor and she thoughtfully stared at the cracks below her feet. She leaned her palm against the edge of the table I was sitting at and placed the notepad against her hip.

"I was really good at all that stuff back then," she said softly to me, not raising her eyes. "I was voted 'Most Likely to Succeed.'"

I remembered. Disdainfully.

She lifted her chin and stared blankly at the boys' table. She blinked her eyes at them as if she forgot what her next move was supposed to be. Finally, she adjusted her apron, jerked a pen loose from the spiral wire of her notepad, and walked away from me. A slow, wide smile formed on her face as she leaned her bosom over one of the boys. She passed her hand gently over his firm, broad shoulder and scribbled his request on her pad.

Chapter 5

It was nighttime when I arrived home from work. I pulled the car up to the curb, and saw Scott sitting in front of the apartment entrance. He was busy flipping the pages of ads he'd likely stolen from my mailbox.

"Remember when I asked you about rent and you told me that everything was included?" I thrust my key into the door lock.

"Yeah..."

"Did that mean you as well?" I threw him a smile so he would know it was meant affectionately. Although, if I had needed to urgently drop a deuce or anything similar that begged for privacy in such a small, quiet place I might not have been so accommodating.

"Am I really here that often?"

I opened the door and smiled. "Do you want anything to eat?"

"Frozen pizza?" He followed me inside and watched quietly as I ripped the frozen pizza packaging apart and collected the extra grated cheese from the wrapper. I turned on the oven to preheat it when my eyes caught a movement through the blinds hanging over the French doors.

"Did someone move in next door?" I asked.

He stared blankly at me.

"Over there," I said. I pointed toward the wall adjoining the two studio apartments.

"Nobody moved in," he said. "Why are you asking?"

My face flushed. "I wanted to see what the inside of the place looked like, so I peeked through the blinds."

"And you saw someone in there?"

I shrugged. "I'm not sure."

"I don't think so," Scott said. "My parents haven't said anything to me. And they would know, even though they don't own it. All the landlords communicate with one another. Anyway, how was your first day of waitressing?"

"Hostessing," I corrected.

He rolled his eyes. "Whatever, my dear."

"Not as much fun as I was hoping," I said. I turned the knob on the oven.

"It's a run-down diner in the middle of nowhere. How much fun did you think you'd be having?"

I shrugged.

"And when did you develop this sudden interest in fun?" he asked.

I filled a kettle with warm water and set it on the stove.

"Sarah?"

"What?"

"How long are you planning on doing this for?" he asked.

"I don't know." I placed my hand near the blue flames from the stove and felt their soothing warmth.

Scott sat down in front of my computer. My open Facebook page was showing on the screen. "How many Facebook friends do you have?"

"Thirty-five," I said.

He made the sound of a buzzer going off. "It says here that you have thirty-three."

I felt my face flush. "No. Really? I should have thirty-five friends on there," I said. I walked up behind him and peered over his shoulder. "*Two* people unfriended me? Since this morning?"

"Nice going, Sarah," Scott said. He stood up and went to the kitchenette. He plunged a spoon into a full jar of honey and dripped it onto his tongue. "What, did you post nude pictures of yourself, or something?" he asked.

"No, I posted nude pictures of you." I smirked.

"Ooh, touché," he said. "I love the sense of security this site gives. Let's see... I'm not on your 'friends' list, because I don't have an account. Does that mean I'm not your 'friend'?" He used air quotes. "Does that mean I don't 'like' you?" He used air quotes again, smiled an open-mouthed, toothy smile, and gave a single thumb up. Then he licked his spoon and threw it carelessly into the sink.

"Can you just search for the name Jen?"

"Why?" he asked. "Who's Jen?"

"She's always posting about how she likes to 'clean house' and get rid of 'dead weight'."

Scott stood up. He shut his eyes, arched his back, and stretched his arms high over his head. "Here's a thought. Why don't you post something like, 'I am so sad today. Two people unfriended me, and I am feeling so alone... and lonely.' Then see how many respond with their heartfelt sympathies. 'I am so sorry to hear that, Sarah...' Or

'hugs...' Or 'thinking of you during this difficult time...'
You can turn a negative into a positive, and go from feeling
rejected to feeling like you are the most popular person on
Earth."

I smiled, throwing a tea bag into a mug.

"I personally think Facebook is a huge government-
funded sociological study on maladaptive human
behavior." Scott traced the rim of the honey jar with the tip
of his finger. He sat back down in front of the computer.
"Let's see... What is Facebook, according to the Internet?
Well, at least according to Yahoo, which, as we all know,
really *is* the Internet because of its high and respectable
standards when it comes to steering away from yellow
journalism... Facebook is a..." He started typing. "The first
thing that automatically comes up when I type 'Facebook is
a...' into the Yahoo search window is 'a waste of time.'
This is followed by 'social network...' which is followed by
'distraction...' which is followed by 'joke...' which is
followed by 'public entity...' which is followed by 'scam...'
which is followed by 'popularity contest...' which is
followed by 'waste of life...' which is followed by 'public
forum... ' which is followed by 'disease'."

"Pastor Paul... I don't know if you remember him from
the church on Main Street?"

"Um... I think so?" he said. "Not sure."

"Well, he once said that the Internet facilitates
communication, but destroys intimacy. He said the Internet
promotes conflict, without resolution."

"Nicely put." He nodded. "I agree. Just sad it has to be that way, with so many people hypnotically drawn to it, to the point where it takes the place of real human contact. Think about just how absurd it is that a soulless subject like that is even brought up in a sermon in a church. It's infiltrated everything."

I heard a thumping noise. "Someone's outside," I said. I moved toward my bed.

Scott walked over to the French doors. He peered through the cracks of the blinds. "It must be the echoes of the tapping feet of carnival freaks and circus clowns bouncing off the inner walls of your skull." He smirked at me, acknowledging that he was being a jackass. "Because I heard nothing. And I see nothing."

"Somebody moved in," I whispered. I walked up behind him.

"There's nobody here," he insisted. He drew the heavy blinds up and opened the doors. A gust of cool air rushed into the studio as he stepped out onto the porch and looked around.

"Get back in here," I said, nervously.

He stumbled inside, closed the French doors, and stared down at the oven. "What setting do you have this on? Sarah..." He shook his head and forcefully twisted the oven dial. He folded his arms and stared down at the dusty cobwebs hanging from the bottom of the kitchen counter.

There was another thump.

Scott's body jerked. He opened the French doors again and slowly stepped onto the porch. I saw a smile on his face as he bent his body down toward the wooden planks below him and lifted a scrawny black cat up into his arms.

"You have milk, right?" he asked. "I mean, *got milk?*" He carried the animal over the threshold of the doorway and opened the refrigerator.

"Two days past the expiration date," I said.

"Check for cottage cheese-like lumps, and then pour a few drops into a bowl of water," he said. He lifted a nearly empty carton lined with a cheesy film around its neck.

"Why do *I* have to?" I asked.

"Because you're the woman."

I handed the carton back to him. "Go blow."

He stroked the cat's neck while it sniffed and licked the dish of milk and water that he prepared for it.

"Scott?"

"Um-hmmm?" he said. He looked affectionately down at the cat.

"What do you know about Pamela?"

"Pamela?" he asked. He poured a drop of spoiled milk into a mug of hot English tea and sat on my bed. "Pamela," he said with a guttural groan, blowing lightly on the surface of his drink. He slurped his tea and then gulped loudly. "I love watching her body move the way it moves."

I felt a queer throbbing in my stomach. It was like someone sucker punched me. I dug my fingers into my skin and tried to soften the hardened mass underneath my rib cage. I bent down, placed my hand between the cat's pointy shoulder blades, and concentrated on stroking its dull fur.

"I can't believe she didn't remember you," Scott said.

"Oh, come on, Scott. Are you out of your mind?" I glanced at the hamsters and watched them running on their wheels, oblivious to the cat's presence. "She remembered me. Unless she has early onset Alzheimer's, how could she not know who I am? We grew up in the same neighborhood and went to the same schools. We graduated less than two years ago."

"You want me to have her killed?" He pulled the steaming pizza out of the oven, momentarily setting off the smoke alarm. "Glad to see this thing really works," he said. He was completely unfazed as he waved a terry cloth beach towel he had grabbed from a rack in the bathroom. The cat's fur stood straight up on its back. It darted quickly under the bed to hide from the piercing noise.

"I hate that thing!" I yelled.

"Saves lives," he said. He tossed the bulky towel on top of a sheet of coffee grounds in the little kitchen sink. "Shortens your life if you have a heart condition, though." He lifted a bed cover off the dusty floor and tried to woo the cat out of hiding. "She had to drop out of college because of some guy she was involved with."

"Uh?" I swallowed a flaming hot piece of pizza whole. "Wuh?" My tongue moved exploringly over a strand of loose, burned flesh behind my front incisors.

He raised his eyebrows and sipped some tea. "There was all this drama with somebody she was dating... She was living with him, actually."

"Who? Or whom, I mean. Or whatever." A drop of saliva slipped off the tip of my tongue and landed on my knee. I quickly wiped my mouth and hoped Scott didn't notice.

"This guy," he said. "Just some guy she knew in college."

"Uh-huh."

"They didn't get along. Always fighting. Out in public." He picked up a slice of pizza and then dropped it suddenly on the counter, waving his fingers in the air as if that would cool them. "Hot!"

"Hmmm..." I took a slow, cautious bite of pizza.

"Hmmm what?"

I quietly chewed the pizza and stared down at my hands.

"Yeah, well, so anyway. I guess things got to be too much for him. And for her. I don't know the details, but something happened. And she dropped out. I think he did, too."

I stopped chewing. "When did this happen?"

"A year ago, I guess? Something like that," Scott said. His eyes lowered to the floor. He was suddenly quiet.

"You all right?" I asked. I leaned toward him and tried to catch his eye.

"No," he mumbled. He shook his head. "I mean, yeah." He looked up at me and shrugged.

"What?" I asked.

"Nothing." He raised his pizza slice to his lips and nibbled on its end. "I'm just..." He looked up at me briefly, and then shook his head again. "Nah..."

"What?" I repeated.

He drew a deep breath and exhaled until there was no more air left in his lungs. "I guess I... feel a little something for her. I don't know."

My stomach lurched. I angrily mashed my fist against it. "Sexual?" I asked.

"Of course sexual!" He cried. He smiled widely at me. "Sexual..." He rolled his eyes. "What else could I have possibly meant? This is *Pamela* we're talking about here." He pinched a piece of pizza crust off his slice and squeezed it between his forefinger and thumb. Then he looked thoughtfully at me. "There's something else, though," he said. "I think it's because she's been through so much. You know? I guess I feel sorry for her. Like I want to take care of her."

You suck, I thought. I pursed my lips and turned my head away from him. I pretended to be interested in watching the cat clean itself by the dish.

"Yeah, I don't know," he said. "She's tried really hard to break into acting. She'd tell me how she'd go on all these auditions, and there would always seem to be someone else who got a call back who she didn't think came close to her talent-wise. She'd joke about how this one or that one got a part the old 'casting couch' way. Well, I mean... she'd say it like she was joking, but I could tell how bitter she really was about it."

"You seem to know an awful lot about her," I said.

"Yeah, well, she talks to me whenever I go to the diner. And honestly, I don't find her story all that different from a lot of people's our age. It's what seems to be the universal worldwide dream: quest for stardom. She's yet another product of media-fueled brainwashing and celebrity worship... instilled unrealistic expectations... universal discontentment with the idea of 'settling' for a regular Joe Sixpack kind of job... I think she thought success would just fall into her lap, like it did in high school, with everyone treating her like she was something special."

"She's something special, all right," I said, thinking about the unfortunate omnipresence of Pamela-like girls, with their stereotypical blond hair and tall, thin builds, catapulted to obscene popularity because of their physical prowess, their over inflated egos haunting the junior high and high school hallways.

He nodded. "Just bizarre how she seems to be giving up so soon. She's only 19, you know?"

I didn't say anything. How could I? I was kind of giving up, too, wasn't I? But unlike Pamela and her post-high school stud aspiration to be unmatched celebrity ruler and queen of the little people, I hardly considered getting a bachelor's degree in the pharmaceutical sciences and eventually a punch the clock job doing lord knows what in some windowless lab somewhere a *dream*. I gave up on something that in retrospect could have been a life sentence. And that was a *good* thing.

Right?

And I sincerely hoped the uncomfortable block of silence between me and Scott wasn't going to serve as a trigger for him to get on his soapbox again. I started rummaging through utensils in one of the kitchen drawers to make background noise just in case.

Scott slapped his knee. "So, Sarah..." He grabbed a piece of pizza, now tepid. He bit into the hardened cheese.

"What?"

"Can you remember the last time you were happy?" he asked.

I leaned over the hamster tank. I watched two balls of fur expand and contract under tattered toilet paper and alfalfa. I lifted the lid off the tank and moved a piece of wood that had gotten wedged between the bars of one of the running wheels.

"You're not answering me," he said.

"I'm too busy thinking about how much you suck," I said, plainly.

He studied my face for a few seconds. He then moved his hand slowly over his nose and mouth and pinched his unshaved chin.

The room grew quiet. I could hear the evening wind gently brushing against the window.

Doug leans his face over my shoulder and watches closely as I cast the tied fly into the water.

"That was good," he says in his high, twelve-year-old voice. "You're gonna catch something. The bait landed in a dark patch. See over there? It's loaded with fish. I know you're gonna get something." He hugs me tightly against his bare, bony chest and stands quietly behind me.

It is our last day together. He leaves for New Hampshire tomorrow with his family. I wonder if this is the last time his father will take him away from friends he barely had time to make.

"Doug?" I say.

"Yeah?"

"Do you have to go?"

"Yeah."

"Will you write me?"

"Sure." He squeezes my arms and points toward the end of my line, which is heavy, taut, and moving.

I turn my face to look at him and I smile. He smiles back, his curly brown hair falling in front of his eyes and partially shading their gleam. He kisses my cheek and helps me reel the fish in.

I reached for the afghan on the bed and flipped its fringes back and forth with my fingertips. "There was a time when I think I was happy." I rested my elbows on the end of my bed and poked my fingers through holes anchoring the fringes.

"What's made you happy?"

"It's not a what. It's a who."

"You're not talking about Gary, are you?" he asked.

"No."

"You mean there's someone else?" he asked.

I nuzzled my face in the afghan. "It was a long time ago. I was just a kid."

"You're still a kid. So it couldn't have been *that* long ago. What happened?"

I slowly sat up. "He moved away." I wrapped the afghan around my shoulders. I felt a sudden draft in the room and pulled the blanket tightly around myself. I stared at him.

"What?" he asked. He looked uncomfortable.

"Nothing," I said, looking away from him.

"What's on your mind?"

I smiled at him and shook my head. "Nothing. I'm just glad you're here."

He snorted and took a bite of his pizza crust. "Can't figure out if I want this or if I don't."

"What?" I asked.

"The pizza crust," he said. "What did you think I meant? Your company?"

"Well, I know I've been moody," I said.

He placed his pointer finger on his chin and looked up at the ceiling as if he were in deep thought. Then he nodded.

"It's character building," I said as I slid off the edge of my bed. I sat on the floor and he joined me. "It grows hair on your chest."

"I've got more than enough character." He pulled at the collar of his shirt to reveal a patch of curly, black hair. "And more sex appeal than I know what to do with."

I glanced away from him. I looked down at the afghan wrapped around me. "I can't get over how much you've changed," I said.

"In what way?"

"You look different now," I said.

"Better or worse?"

I turned to face him. "More mature."

He raised his eyebrows at me and smiled.

"A little more handsome," I said.

"Impossible!"

I leaned my head against his shoulder. "I honestly don't know what I would have done if I didn't have you to run to."

"You would have walked," he said.

I lifted my head up and leaned away. "I wouldn't have come here if you weren't here."

"You wouldn't have?"

"No."

He leaned forward and began picking at his thumb cuticle. "Do you have a nail file or scissors or something?"

I shook my head.

He sucked on the tip of his nail and then looked at me out of the corner of his eyes. "I hate hangnails." He paused to study the damage he had done with all the picking. "Do you know a hangnail is also called 'a stepmother's blessing'?"

I shook my head.

"Isn't that weird?" he asked.

I nodded.

"Yeah." His lips were pressed against the side of his thumb.

"So I've been doing a lot of writing lately," I said. "I'm working on a short story right now, for children."

"Kids love fart humor," he said.

I stared at him.

He looked back at me, licking the side of his thumb. "Well, they *do*!"

I stood up and reached for my manila folder. I opened it and leafed through some loose papers, searching.

"You going to read something to me?" he asked.

"Yeah." I found what I was looking for. "It was Halloween night, many, many moons ago. I sat down on the bench in front of my house, my brand new witch's costume partly hidden beneath my down coat."

"Woo-hoo, a Halloween story. Right up my alley," he said.

I continued. "Crisp night winds blew against the black masquerade mask that covered my face from the bridge of my nose up to my forehead; they made me shiver.

"I heard the footsteps of my older sister, Amy, in the front parlor. The footsteps were soon followed by the sound of the front door opening and closing.

"'OK,' Amy said. 'Let's go.'

"With one hand, I grabbed hold of the edge of my sister's soft, woolen sweater, and with my free arm I swung a plastic container shaped like a gutted pumpkin to and fro."

Scott suddenly gasped. "Ow! Damn it!"

"What?" I asked, lowering the paper, annoyed, dejected.

"I think I tore it," he said, standing and heading into my bathroom. He grabbed some toilet paper and wrapped it around his thumb.

"Do you want me to read this later?" I asked. "When you're less distracted?" *Damn you.*

He carefully lifted the toilet paper off his thumb and examined it. "It's bleeding," he said. "No, continue."

I sighed. "OK. 'Amy?' I asked. 'I heard there's a man who lives on the moon. I also heard that the moon is made of cheese.'

"Amy had been partly listening to me, and partly making sure to safely cross the street with my hand held tightly in her own.

"'Doesn't the cheese get moldy, being outside for so long?'

"'I guess so,' Amy said distantly, crooning her neck to...'"

Scott put his hand up suddenly. "Stop," he said. "Unless you are going to segue into something about cutting the cheese, you've already lost half your audience."

I continued, ignoring him. "My head was still turned up toward the sky when Amy and I neared a set of cobblestone steps leading to an oil lantern-lit doorway. A little old lady appeared under the light holding a large pewter dish loaded with gold- and silver-wrapped chocolates."

Scott started fake snoring.

"I grabbed a handful of candy, smiled quickly up at the woman, and dropped my treats into my plastic pumpkin. I then turned my attention once again to the cold, autumn night sky."

He snored louder.

"Would you *please stop*?" I whined.

"Could you?" He threw his blood-stained tourniquet into the trash.

I hung my head. "So you don't like my writing?" I asked.

He placed his hands on his hips. "It's not that I don't like your writing, Sarah. You write really well," he said. "Your Halloween piece just isn't grabbing me, that's all."

"It's for kids," I argued.

"I'm a kid. A big kid in an adult's body. I'm your perfect test audience." He turned to the kitchen sink and started running cold water on his thumb.

"Whatever," I mumbled.

"Come on, Sarah. You want to be a writer? Especially *now*, in the era of the Internet? Get used to having your work criticized. And get used to seeing anonymous comments about how much your writing sucks, and how much you suck along with it."

"Well I guess I've been groomed for it," I said. "Since people have been telling me I suck my whole life."

"Hey, how about this?" He turned back to face me. "A kid is walking along, right? He starts wondering about something he heard. Is it true that if a person sneezes, farts, and hiccups at the same time, they turn into a black hole? Or would they simply explode?"

I quietly folded my story in half and placed it back in the manila folder.

"Or," he continued. "Do they need to *belch,* fart and hiccup to turn into a black hole? Or... *explode'?*" He raised his finger in the air and started nodding in silent agreement with himself. "This would make an *awesome* picture book!"

"You need to head out now?" I asked, not so subtly hinting.

"Yeah." He gently lifted the cat up into his arms.

Thank God. I opened the side entrance door for him.

"This one's coming with me," he said. "I take in strays. Or, in this case, I take them out." He carried the cat over the doorway threshold and turned to look at me once more before disappearing out of view.

Chapter 6

It was past midnight. Something jolted me awake. *The hamsters*, I thought. I strained my eyes to see past the darkness into their tank. The sounds of their burrowing and scampering melted together with the pitter-patter of water droplets hitting the porch and windows.

A shadow slowly displaced streaks of moonlight sneaking past the lower portion of the French door blinds. I heard a tapping noise. Was it the hamsters' tiny feet striking cedar chips and metal bars? Was it water rushing through bends in the pipes in the walls? As the tapping continued, I realized it was coming from the direction of the shadow, which was still there.

The hamsters stopped foraging and stood still in the middle of their tank. My hands and arms were trembling. I clutched my blanket and dug my feet into the mattress. The shadow quickly disappeared from the patio, leaving behind only the sound of the pouring rain.

I jumped to my feet. There was no way I would be able to get back to sleep. And there was no way I was going to even attempt to try. I pulled on a pair of sweat pants, and shoved my nightshirt inside of them. I grabbed a pair of sneakers out from underneath my bed and stood with them dangling from my fingertips. What was I doing?

I looked over at the French doors, which remained shadow-free. The porch was quiet. But there was enough adrenaline racing through me to power a high speed

locomotive. I had to do something with the energy... even if
it meant channeling it into a completely bonehead move
like leaving the apartment. I slowly inched toward my
closet and pulled the light bulb cord, grabbing a jacket with
still shaking hands.

I raced outside to my car, feeling the rain beating hard
against my scalp and trickling down the sides of my head. I
scraped the car key against the metal surrounding the door
lock, scratching off some paint. I gave the key one final
thrust, pulled hard on the door, and climbed fast into the
front seat.

I squinted through the rain. The porch was empty. I
slowly started the ignition, keeping my eyes fixed on the
apartment.

I then heard a light tapping sound on the driver's side
window. I froze. I swallowed hard. I quickly shifted into
drive and steered the car away from the curb, driving fast
toward the intersecting main roadway. I could see in my
rearview mirror a dripping figure in a long, dark coat,
standing near where my car had been.

A mile or so away was the Willow Branch, a small
tavern with soft, orange light streaming through its
windows. I walked inside and shook drops of rain out of
my hair.

"Sarah."

It was Pamela's voice. I turned my head toward the
large, wooden table she was sitting at, leering at me with
droopy eyelids. She was facing a man, obviously a hunter

in a camouflage jacket and heavy boots, who was seated on a nearby bar stool.

I watched beads of water fall off the top of my head and onto the wooden floor below me.

"Raining out?" Pamela said with a smile. She motioned for the bartender to prepare two of whatever it was she had been drinking. "You look like you just saw a ghost," she said.

"Someone was at my apartment," I said. "Someone knocked on my door, woke me up, scared me half to death."

She shrugged. "All right. Calm down," she said sluggishly. She shook her head in disgust. "Have a drink." Using her chin, she pointed to a Southern Comfort the bartender had set down in front of me.

I gulped the burning liquor down until the glass was empty. "Excuse me," I said. I turned briskly around. My fingertips were numb. I dialed the police on my cell phone and asked for a car to patrol the neighborhood.

I turned around, ready to head back to the table. I noticed that Pamela had started talking again with the man at the bar. As I approached her, she waved her hand quickly at him and made exaggerated hushing noises with her mouth.

"What?" I asked.

Pamela smiled. She looked like she was suppressing a laugh.

"What?" I asked again.

"Nothing," she said, still smiling. She turned to her friend and mouthed something to him that I couldn't hear.

The patron's face flushed and he raised his eyebrows. He lifted the full glass of Southern Comfort that sat in front of her and placed it back on the bar. "Play nicely," he said.

"I am, Elmer," she said.

Elmer? As in Fudd? I started to walk away. Pamela motioned for me to come back to the table. "Look, look, Sarah. Let's just drink and be marry. I mean..." She started laughing loudly again and slapped her hand hard on Elmer's arm. "Did you hear what I said? I said, '*marry*'! Do you believe it? Was that a Freudian slip or *what*?"

I hesitantly leaned back toward the table. I waited for her laughter to die down. "I have a question," I said.

"What's that?" She stood up and playfully tried reaching for the drink Elmer set back down on the bar. He lightly grasped her wrists and moved her back in her seat.

I waited until she was sitting somewhat still and facing me again. "It's a favor," I said.

"A favor!" She launched again into loud, raucous laughter.

"Please listen to me?" I asked.

"Sure," she said. She made a half-hearted attempt to compose herself.

"I want you to apologize."

She stared wide-eyed at me. "Why? For what?" she asked. Her lips were pressed tightly together, seeming to suppress more laughter.

"Why?" I echoed. "For what," I said. All of a sudden I wasn't able to remember the meaning of the words. "You know why." I wrinkled my forehead.

"We were *kids*..." she said.

"Yeah, I know that."

"We're not kids anymore."

"That's not an apology," I said.

"It wasn't meant to be one."

I stared down at the table. "This isn't going anywhere. Just forget it."

"No!" she shouted. "You have a problem with me. Let's talk about it." I knew she wasn't being sincere. She didn't want a discussion. She wanted a fight.

"There's nothing to talk about," I said, "if you can't handle something as simple as what I want."

"Oh, I can *handle* it," she said, venomously. "It's too bad you can't seem to handle *life*."

I stood up again and started walking away from the table. "You've had too much to drink."

"Sarah!" she shouted at me.

I quietly stood in place. I stared in her direction but didn't look into her eyes.

"Why are you trying to make me feel guilty... over something that happened such a long time ago?"

I tried to suppress my anger. "I'm trying to let you know that you did things to me that really *affected* me. And not in a good way."

She stared down toward the table. Her hands were tightly clasped. "I personally think you should be apologizing to yourself."

"*What*?"

"For always being the victim," she said, smirking. "Spineless. You didn't have to be, but you were. You really have no one to blame but yourself."

I felt all the blood in my body climb toward my neck and crawl up my face. I rushed toward the table and squeezed my fingers around her folded hands. "Just an apology!" I yelled. "That's all I'm asking for! And you can't do it!" I dug my fingers more forcefully into the loose skin between her knuckles.

"Get off of me!" She tried to writhe out of my grasp. Elmer stood up and pulled me away from her.

The bartender, wiping pools of beer on the counter, gave us a concerned look. "Is everything OK?" he called.

"So far," the man called back. He glanced first at me, then at Pamela.

I sat back down in my chair. My eyes felt like the eyes of an insect, bulging out of my head.

"Why are you doing this?" Pamela asked. Her face was flushed and her eyes glossy with fatigue.

I stared at her. Silent.

She rubbed her red knuckles. "We have to work together. With my sen... seniority, and the fact... that you just started, do you know how fast I could get you fired?"

"It helps to be in the boss's good embraces," I said. "Er. I mean graces." I sat up straight in my chair.

She lunged across the table to swing at me. But she lost her balance, and the corner of the table pushed hard into her stomach. She grabbed the wood tightly, leaned partly over the table's edge and started to hyperventilate. Quickly, she raised her head and ran to the lavatory.

Elmer shifted uncomfortably on the bar stool. He lowered his head.

I looked up at him.

He coughed into his fist. "You know," he said, "she told me earlier she was about to get engaged."

I peered over at the ladies room. It was very quiet.

"I really don't know the guy, but he seems all right. At least for her," he said.

"Is he from around here?"

"Work's over at Jay's Liquor," he said. "Comes in here once in a while."

My face paled. I blinked hard.

"Everything all right?" he asked.

I shook my head. I stared into his eyes and continued to blink unnaturally. "What's his name?"

He paused and ran his fingers over his mouth. "Gary."

"*What is it?*"

He twirled his nearly empty beer bottle on the counter. "It's Gary. I think he's Jay's boy."

We heard a toilet flush and saw the door of the lavatory slowly open. With her eyes fixed on the floor, Pamela walked over to the closest bar stool and sat down.

"You OK, hun?" Elmer asked. He put his arm around her.

"Yes," she said, quietly. She glared at me out of the corners of her eyes for a moment. Then she turned toward the bartender. "Sorry," she said softly to him.

Elmer stood. "If you'll excuse me, now that I know you're all right, I've got to get home." He gathered his hunting gear and waved to the bartender.

Pamela took tiny sips from a glass of ice water the bartender had set down in front of her. Wincing, she said, "My stomach is really upset."

I cleared my throat. "I'm sorry," I said.

She looked at me with narrowed eyes. "No need to *apologize*." She threw some money on the bar, and pulled the hood of her raincoat over her head.

I sat motionless as she left. I was exhausted. I just wanted to crawl into my warm, dry bed and cry. Only I was too scared to leave.

"Shouldn't you be home? Sleeping or something?" the bartender asked.

I nodded.

"Can I get you anything?"

"Do you have tea?" I asked.

"One tea," he said, walking away.

I tapped softly on the splintery table top. "Can I ask you something?" I called to him.

"Sure." He poured boiled water into a mug containing an Earl Grey tea bag, and tossed some containers of cream and packets of sugar on the bar.

"How well do you know Pamela?"

He looked at me curiously. "She's a regular here."

"Do you know anything about her boyfriend?"

"Gary?" he said. He started to sweep the dusty floor. "He comes in here sometimes."

The tea was scorching hot. I sipped slowly on it, its warmth gradually lulling me to sleep. I rested my head on my hands and closed my eyes.

I'm standing in a large wheat field. I am twirling as fast as I can in the center of many tall, swaying shafts of wheat and watching the sky turning with me. I stop all at once and happily anticipate the rest of the world also coming to a sudden stop.

In the midst of the blur I see a tall, willowy, feminine form that appears to be standing in the field with me. As everything around me settles down, I see that it is Pamela. She is posed a short distance away with a smile on her face and a matchbook in her hands. She launches into a series of cartwheels and lands right next to me, lighting a match and setting the wheat surrounding me on fire. Still smiling, she bends her body forward, propels herself toward the sky and continues to soar high over the burning wheat field.

I feel the warmth of the fire intensify until my skin becomes red and swollen. I run quickly, flailing my arms and trying to catch her legs as she playfully dives in and out of the growing flames. She turns her head to face me.

She is laughing now.

I jerked my head up from the bar in a swift motion, painfully pulling a muscle in my neck. Rubbing my shoulder, I turned to see the bartender standing behind the counter serving rum and Coke to a late night arrival. I lifted my hands to rub my eyes. A flier advertising new drinks available at the tavern fell from the sleeve of my tucked-in nightshirt. I yawned, slipped into my raincoat, and walked outside.

The early morning air was thick and moist, a light drizzle in front of a glowing green sign with the tavern's name. I opened my car door and jumped back as a field mouse ran past my feet in the mud and hid near the front tire. Once I had started the engine with a shaky hand, I quickly backed the car away from the tavern. I hoped I didn't flatten the rodent.

My street was still and quiet when I pulled up. I shut the engine off and stared for a few moments at the dim yellow light shining from the street lamps on the wet pavement. I listened to the light rain drumming against the car hood. The neighboring studio was as black and silent as my own.

Once inside, I ran to my bed. I pulled the covers up to my chin and nervously glanced all around me. I closed my eyes and tried to fall asleep, yet my overtired mind kept me awake.

I'm standing by a row of lockers in tenth grade gym class. I'm fumbling with my lock and growing anxious because it will not open, though I'm sure I am using the right combination. Time is ticking away, and most of the girls have already left the locker room to sit on their designated painted numbers on the gymnasium floor. I see a pair of shorts on a bench on the other side of the room. I notice a group of girls standing in a huddled mass. I walk over to them.

I clear my throat. "Do these belong to anybody?" I hold the shorts up for everyone to see.

The girls turn around to look at me. Pamela is among them. With a lit cigarette poking out from behind her, she approaches me.

"Why?" she asks.

"I can't get my locker open. I need clothes for class."

"Those are mine," she says. She uses her chin to point to the shorts. "They're my only pair."

I look at the lower half of her body, already clad in another pair of gym shorts. I stare past her at the group of girls. "Does anyone have an extra pair of shorts I can borrow?" I ask.

The girls stare at me, expressionless. A couple of them look at each other and smirk, but no one answers me.

Pamela grabs her shorts and pushes me, causing me to stumble and fall to the floor. She kneels down beside me and whispers, "You're a loser who can't remember three simple numbers." She walks back to her friends with a trail of smoke lagging behind her. I hear her laughing.

That night, I tossed and turned under my blanket. I pulled the pillow over my head and clenched my teeth. Finally, I stopped flipping from side to side and lay completely still, staring solemnly up at the ceiling. The sound of water pounding the marshy ground invaded my mind. My breathing grew slower and deeper until at long last I fell asleep.

Chapter 7

"What are you doing here?" I called from the curb.

"Meditating," Scott said. He was leaning against the edge of my porch.

I hustled past him and thrust the key into the lock.

He stood up. He slapped the dust off his trousers. "What's up?"

I pushed hard on the door, making it bounce against the inner wall. I angrily marched inside.

Scott's head slowly emerged from behind the doorway. "Can I come in?" he asked. "Should I come in? Should I leave? *Can* I leave?"

I didn't say anything.

"What's wrong?" he asked, unable to abandon me.

I fell backward onto the bed. I rested the back of my wrist on my forehead.

Scott gripped both sides of his head with his hands and tugged at his hair with mild exasperation. "I can count the number of days you've been here on my fingers. What could possibly have gone so wrong in this short amount of time?"

"I hate those doors," I said, pointing. "Those supposedly safe doors."

"Why?" he asked.

"Someone was knocking on them last night," I said.

"Did you see who it was?" He opened the kitchen cabinet, looked around, and shut it.

90

"The Avon Lady," I said.

He rinsed out a dirty cup and poured some warm soda into it. "If it happens again, call me. OK?"

"I called the police."

"They're useless," he said. He took a sip from the cup and grimaced. "Feh! This is completely flat!" He poured it down the drain. "You want to go to Angel Rock with me tonight?"

I raised an eyebrow. "Do you want me to throw up all over you?"

"Come on..." he said. "Angel Rock Leap. I thought you loved that place."

"It's forever tarnished," I said, melodramatically.

"You're stuck in the past again... the crappy part. Let's make new memories there. We can grab a pizza on the way. Let's go." He clutched my upper arm and tried to lift me up off the bed. "Pizza. OK? Come on. Seriously. Let's go."

"Scott?"

"What?"

"Why didn't you tell me about Pamela and Gary?" I asked.

"What about them?"

"You know..."

"Know what?" he asked. His feet slid under the bed while I grasped the mattress and tried to resist his efforts to shift me. His legs and hips followed his feet and he lay on the floor, the bed covering half of his body.

"Don't play dumb."

"You left. Did your thing. Why do you care what other people do?" He grabbed the bottom edge of the bed and lifted himself up.

"I'm working with her," I said. "And I dated *him*."

"OK, so now you know," he said. He took my hand and tugged at it hard, pulling me to my feet. "Let's just go, huh?"

* * * *

We walked quietly along a twisting, hilly road, passing a six pack of soda back and forth. Scott kept opening a warm box of pizza and popping pepperoni slices into his mouth as we walked along the main roadway.

The sky had changed from a rich auburn to a dark gray as we hugged the pebbly roadside. A familiar landmark in the distance became clearer to me, and I squinted to see if the old, splintery wooden sign saying "Little Ducklings" was still intact after all these years. It sat under the yellow glow of a tall neon lamp and pointed to the other side of the road at a small day care center. The ravine was hidden away several yards behind the sign, comfortably nestled at the base of a lengthy dirt path.

We heard voices as we made our way down the bumpy trail. As we drew nearer, I could see the shadows of two people moving in front of a distant pile of burning twigs. They were sitting on flattened limestone surrounded by water, and basking in the small gusts of warmth coming from the nearby fire.

"No," Scott moaned. "This was supposed to be ours tonight."

"Who's there?" I whispered.

"Why? Who cares?" Scott whispered back.

I tiptoed through fallen branches and crackling leaves, pushing past the trunks of sugar maples lining our path. I felt Scott's hot breath against my neck. I motioned with my hand for him to give me some space and accidentally slapped him on his cheek.

"What's your *problem*?" he whispered, holding his face.

"Sorry," I whispered back, squinting to see through the dark. I watched the silhouette of a woman stand up and kick her legs over her head, remaining gracefully suspended in the air. She landed lightly on her knees, laughed heartily, and threw her arms around the man. "I'm still hung over," I could hear her say in between giggles.

Scott quietly sat down behind a rose bush, popped the lid of the cardboard box up and shoved a slice of pizza into his mouth. He soundlessly drew the melted cheese on the pizza slice up between his lips and loudly licked the grease and crumbs up from his fingertips.

"This is too much," I whispered. I took a seat next to Scott and watched him eat, feeling too sick myself to even swallow.

It was too quiet. We could see them and hear them too clearly. A part of me wanted to leave. A bigger part of me, though, forced me to stay. I silently cursed the bigger part of me.

Pamela stroked Gary's hair and leaned her face in close to his ear.

"You're so beautiful," he said. There was a quaver in his voice. It was followed by silence.

"And?"

He put his fingers against her mouth for a second. "Pam..."

"Yes?"

There was another long pause.

"Gary, honey? What is it?"

There was a stillness.

"What is it?" she repeated.

"I..."

"What?"

"Could you stop interrupting me?" he asked, sounding mildly annoyed.

She drew away from him.

"I'm confused," he said.

She looked at him.

"I don't know... if things, maybe, could be more... right for me. Or for you," he said.

"I don't believe this!" she yelled. Her echo bounced off surrounding wave-polished stones.

"Pam, please."

"Please what?" she asked. She stood up and moved away from him. "You brought me out here."

"Pam..."

She buried her face in her hands and started to cry.

"I need time," he said. "That's all I'm trying to say to you." He put his hand on her shoulder.

"For what?" she asked, sniffling.

"I just need some time..."

"Time for *what*?"

"I don't know. To figure out if you and I are really meant for each o..."

"Stop!" she yelled.

"I just wanted to tell y..."

"Stop!" She started to pace back and forth.

"Pamela?" Gary said, reaching out to her.

"Stop!" she screamed, holding her finger up to his face. "Don't..." She threw her arms down and stepped off the rock. She hopped over some stones and stood by the dying fire.

"Pamela..." Gary continued to keep his arm outstretched, walking toward her. His hand suddenly fell and hung lethargically in front of his leg. A light wind tousled the leaves on surrounding hickory trees and gently rocked their branches. Gary squatted and stared at his feet while Pamela stood statuesque by the fire.

"You know Sarah's back," she said.

"Sarah?"

"From high school," she said.

He looked at her and didn't say anything.

She hopped from the smoldering fire and leaped back onto the rock Gary stood on.

"Did you hear me?" she asked.

"Yes. I didn't know," he said.

She pressed her nose up against the tip of his. "I'm sure," she said. She pushed into him, causing him to stumble backwards and submerge his ankles in a shallow pool of water. She sprinted up the dirt path, breathing heavily and crushing the open lid of the pizza box on her way. She didn't see us as she hurried past.

Gary skipped over some stones and reached the wooded area where the fire was lit. He crouched down by its side and began breaking off pieces of twigs and throwing them into the dying flames. He stood up slowly and stared down at the embers with his arms folded tightly across his chest. With a heavy sigh, he turned and headed sluggishly over the rocks and up the trail.

I clenched Scott's shoulders and buried my head in his back as Gary walked past. He stopped short near us and quickly turned around.

"Scott?" he said. He moved closer and squinted. "Sarah?"

We both stood.

"I don't believe this," Gary said. He shook his head and started to walk away.

"Wait, Gary... Here. Have a ginger ale," Scott said, holding a can out to him.

Gary ignored him. "Sarah..." he said.

Even in the dark, I could still see the vibrant blue of his eyes.

Instead of continuing to wait for me to say something, Gary looked down at his feet and walked back toward some jagged-edged limestone jutting out of the water. "What are you guys doing here?"

Scott hopped onto a rock and tried handing him another can of soda. "Having a tough time of it, huh?"

Gary shrugged. He pushed the can away. "I think you already know the answer to that. Could you do something about the fire?" He held a weathered book of matches out to Scott. "It's getting too dark to see."

"No problem," Scott said. He ran over to the smoky pile of branches and twigs.

Gary lit a match from another worn book and held it up to where I was standing. "You still look the same," he mumbled, shaking the flame away. His eyes glistened in the firelight as if filling with tears. He swept his glance away from me and focused on the soda can, still in Scott's hands. "I really do care about her," he said.

From the fireside, I saw Scott roll his eyes at me.

"Really do," Gary said, staring thoughtfully into the woods.

I stood up and began walking toward the dirt path. I did not look at either of them.

"Hey!" Scott yelled. "Where are you going?"

"Home," I said.

"Come back, Sarah!" Scott ran over to me and grabbed my arm.

"Let's leave him alone," I said. I turned to look at Gary. He was slumped over and ogling the ground under his feet.

"Wait up... I'll go with you," Scott said. He grabbed the remaining soda cans and the crushed pizza box, and jogged closely behind me.

I walked swiftly along the road, listening to the clanking of soda cans and the shuffling of cold pizza slices on cardboard behind me.

"Sarah?" he asked.

"Make it quick."

"Why are you running?"

"Why do you think?" I kicked a ball of dust off the pavement below and sighed. "Too many people are making me feel like not a day has gone by since I last saw them," I said. "And that would be OK if things didn't completely suck... the last time I saw them."

"What did you expect by coming back here?" he asked. We were about to pass his parents' apartment.

I shivered and pressed my arms closer to my chest. "It really is like time's stood still."

Scott bent over his empty trash can and threw the pizza box inside. "You want these?" he asked, lifting two full soda cans up in the air.

"No."

He opened his mailbox and set the cans inside. He then took my arm in his and pulled me away from the sidewalk leading to his apartment. "We're going for a walk."

I moved in an attempt to break free from his grip. "I'm really cold, Scott," I said. "Let me go home."

"There's somewhere I want to go first." He continued pulling me further away from the neighborhood.

We passed the Willow Branch and continued down a long, straight road. It was flanked by sparse halogen lamps and weed-strewn meadows. I knew exactly where the road would lead to, yet I couldn't understand why Scott had chosen that of all places to visit.

"Why?" I asked, stumbling as I tried to keep up with him.

He walked a little faster. He pulled me by the elbow until we reached a tall black metal fence that enclosed grassy knolls dotted with tombstones. Scott gently placed his hands on my shoulders and made the back of my neck turn cold and bumpy.

"Why are we here?" I asked.

"This place relaxes me," he said, taking a seat by a gravestone shaped like a harp. "I was hoping it would have the same effect on you."

"You're creepy," I said.

"I can't help myself. Drawn as I am to the dark side."

I trailed my hand across the rough, curved surface of a headstone. "I have family members here," I said, sitting down on the ground. I plucked a blade of grass and began to peel it down the middle.

He looked down at his feet, and quietly hung his head. "I've got a closet full of books to lend you," he said, suddenly.

"I don't feel like reading anything," I said. I waved my hand carelessly.

"These'll get you going."

"How so?"

"Sarah..." he said. "This is stuff you've got to read. These books describe all these local hauntings people have witnessed... dating back to the Civil War. You can't *not* read this."

"I can't, huh? Why?"

"Because it's fascinating."

I shook my head.

He shrugged. "And... honestly?" He paused. "Quite honestly, I want to believe that maybe there's more to all this than just life and death," he said. "Reading these stories... It gives me some kind of... hope. That it's not all completely over... you know... when it's over."

I lay down and rested my head on the ground. I watched a cloud drift slowly past the moon.

He moved toward me on his knees and rested on his side. "So Sarah..."

"What?"

"If I were you..." he said. "I'd make a special effort to try to be happy."

"Why?"

"Because... most of the ghost stories I've read have been about these tortured souls who manifested their unhappiness by pestering the hell out of the living." He lay flat on his back and crossed his arms over his rib cage. "I'm working to make the future world a safer place. Trying to protect people here."

I grabbed a handful of grass from the ground and threw it at him.

He slowly sat up and placed his hand over his mouth as though contemplating something deep and profound. "Sarah... You sad, little hair-entangled dust ball of gloominess... sucked up in the gigantic Hoover vacuum cleaner of life."

Another fierce wind blew by, making cocoons of fall webworms sway on a nearby walnut tree. Scott clasped his fingers around his short, curly pony tail and blew a stream of air out of his mouth.

There was a small metal bench near the main trail. I pointed to it and motioned for him. More gusts of chilly air tousled my hair as I sat down. I watched the blades of grass surrounding the tombstones bend in unison as the wind squirmed through them. I saw Scott out of the corner of my eye looking at me as he sat down.

I drummed my fingertips on the back of the bench and turned my head toward him. I nudged his arm with my shoulder. "What do you really think of me?" I asked, staring at him.

He gazed down into my eyes with his mouth partly open like he was about to say something. He pulled at his collar with his forefinger and then scratched his head. "I think you're someone who needed to be hugged more as a child."

I was quiet. I looked over at the webworm cocoons, draped mercilessly over some tree branches. "I just want to know what you think of me," I said.

"In what respect?"

"Any respect. I just want to know what your impression is."

He cleared his throat and said, "I... think you're an extremely nice person. Neurotic, but nice."

"Uh-huh," I said, resting my chin on my chest. "Tell me something else."

"So you're fishing," he said, his voice sounding strained.

"Well I don't want you to lie, or anything. Just tell me what you think of me."

"I just did!"

"Tell me what you think of me... as a woman," I said.

He pretended to wipe invisible beads of sweat off his forehead. "We're venturing into a minefield here. Sarah..."

"What?"

"We're friends. I can't think of someone who's my really close friend as a... *woman*."

"Pretend like we're strangers."

He sighed. "Sarah, I can't."

I was dying for a compliment. But apparently I was going to be left to gasp and sputter and flop around like the waterless fish I was feeling like at that moment. *Thanks, Scott.* "So you can't even pretend, huh..."

"What are you *doing* to me?"

I was silent. On the outside. Inside, I was screaming at my unbelievably fragile ego to buck up.

Scott swept his hand over his mouth and nodded his head. "You're fine, Sarah."

Not what I was looking for. *Fine.* A dying, gasping, sputtering, waterless fish is fine too if you're planning on frying it for dinner. *Just fry me already, Scott.*

He shrugged. "I said you're *fine*. There's nothing wrong with you."

"I'm fine," I repeated. I felt the crimson creeping up my neck and cheeks.

"Do you want to start heading back now?" he asked. "I'm getting a little tired." He stood and stretched.

"Scott?"

"Whaaat?"

"If we weren't such good friends, and notice I'm using the big 'if' here... would you..."

"Oh, please," he said. "Don't ask me that."

"Don't ask you what? You don't know what I was going to say."

"I know what you were going to say, Sarah," he said. "Why are you asking me all of these bizarre questions?"

"I just want to know if..."

"You want to know if I find you attractive enough to want to become romantically involved with you," he said.

I glanced quickly at his face and then down at my feet.

"It's this kind of talk that's been known to ruin really strong friendships," he said.

I nodded.

"So why are you pushing?"

"I don't know," I said.

He started to walk away from me. He suddenly stopped and turned to face me again. "Sarah, I'm really particular when it comes to women."

I stared down at my feet. "Selective," I said.

"Particular," he corrected, after a pause.

I continued looking down. "So what... *particularly*... are you looking for?"

He pinched his chin. "Someone with... Let's see... Small facial features. A sleek build. Long legs... I love long legs." He made a slurping sound.

"Sounds like you're describing Pamela," I said.

He chuckled. But he didn't deny it.

"You're talking about somebody's physical appearance. Is that all that's important to you?" I asked.

He shook his head. "No."

"I see." I blinked a few times at him. I slowly stood up and started to walk in the direction of the cemetery gate.

"What?" he asked. "What did I say?" He jogged toward me and lightly punched my arm. "Sarah, you and I... we're *friends*. Doesn't that mean anything to you?"

I continued to walk away from him.

"Sarah, what's going on?"

I moved quickly past the rows of tombstones lining the main cemetery trail. "Just leave me alone."

"Sarah!" Scott yelled. He ran after me. "Sarah! I'm sorry for... I don't know! Whatever!"

I didn't turn around.

"Sarah! Come on!" he yelled from the distance, slowing his pace.

I quickly turned onto a dark side street. I squatted behind an overgrown shrub and waited for him to pass by. I lowered my head and cried softly, muffling the sounds with the palms of my hands.

I heard the rustling of grass nearby and swiftly wiped the tears from my eyes. I kept my head pointed toward the pair of feet that planted themselves in front of my bent knees. I reluctantly took the hand that was dangled in front of my face. He tightly gripped my waist, and I kept my eyes closed while he stroked my hair and rested his cheek on the top of my head.

Rarely had I ever been this close to him before. I was surprised by the slightly stale, somewhat musty scent of his clothes. Breathing in deeply, I squeezed him as tightly as he was squeezing me. Yet as I held onto him, I noticed that his body seemed fuller than I would have otherwise expected it to have been. He was also taller.

Much taller.

My fingers swept past the fabric of a stiff, wool coat as I embraced him. He had been wearing a t-shirt.

I broke away as fast as my feet would allow me to, tripping over them at one point and almost falling to the ground. A distance away, I saw the green fluorescent sign in front of the Willow Branch. Once reaching it, I quickly walked through the tavern door, half-expecting to see Pamela hunched over the bar with a stiff drink in her hands. Yet I only saw a handful of men scattered about the room, turning toward me in unison. A couple of them continued to stare as I made my way across the peanut shell-garnished hardwood floor. Had I not been traumatized, I might have found this flattering.

I ordered a glass of Coke at the far end of the bar. I would have asked for a shot of rum or whiskey or something of a similar vein to calm my nerves, but in addition to not being a fan of alcohol, I also didn't want to conform too much to the "local" small town mentality. They could keep their incessant cigarette smoking, as well.

My hand started to tremble as I lifted the glass to my lips, and I looked up to see if anyone was watching me. My eyes met those of a young man with a crew cut sitting a couple of bar stools away.

He stepped down from the bar and, keeping his head bent toward the floor, walked slowly toward me. He shyly glanced up at me once he reached the end of the counter and cleared his throat. "How are you?"

"I'm fine," I answered, shakily. "How are you?" I kept glancing at the tavern door.

"Oh, pretty good." He paused for a moment. "You have no idea who I am, do you?"

I looked hard at his face. "Brian?"

He smiled.

"I didn't recognize you," I said. "Your hair is so much shorter now."

"Yeah, well, it's still me," he said, running his hand through the stubble on his head.

I forced myself to continue smiling. "It's good to see you again."

"Yeah... I'm surprised to see you back. Are you just visiting, or..."

"No," I interrupted. "I moved back here just a little while ago."

He chuckled. "Farthest I've ever gotten away from this place is Newburgh."

I nodded. I was feeling a little calmer. "So what are you doing now?"

He shoved his hands in his pockets and placed his foot on a brass foot rail sticking out of the bottom of the counter. He chuckled. "I'm working in a pet store."

"Why are you laughing?" I asked.

"'Cause it was one of those things that was just supposed to bring in extra pocket money while I was going to college. Now, it's all I do. I quit school."

"Oh," I said. I peered down at my drink and traced the rim of my glass with my forefinger.

"Aah, I shouldn't complain." He leaned his weight against the counter. "I'm manager of the shop now."

I looked up at his face. There was an uncomfortable silence. The background barroom chatter could barely be heard. I fixed my gaze on my half-empty glass of Coke.

A group of us are standing around near a wire fence, waiting for the high school coach to arrive so our co-ed softball game can begin. Dawn and I separate ourselves from the other students and sit down on a nearby bench.

I jump when a softball is thrown and loudly vibrates the fence behind us. Turning around, I see Pamela tossing a ball up and down in her hand and preparing herself to throw it toward us. Dawn and I stand up and leap away from the fence as the ball hits it.

"Look at them flinch," Pamela loudly says to her friends as she points her finger at us.

I feel all of the blood in my body rush up to my cheeks.

"Are you scared?" she asks me.

I remain silent.

"Are you scared?" she repeats, walking over to where I am standing. She pushes my shoulder with her hand. "Answer me. Are you scared?"

"Why don't you leave her alone?" Dawn says, wedging her body in between Pamela and myself.

"Who are you to talk?" Pamela says.

I move a few steps away from both of them and quietly take a seat on the bench. Pamela gives Dawn a daring look and walks over to where I am sitting.

"You want to fight?" she asks.

"No," I say, turning my head away from her.

She grabs my arm and pulls me to my feet. "Come on!"

I notice Brian standing a few feet away from us, observing everything that is taking place. My eyes meet his, and he looks away.

The coach finally arrives and begins handing out gloves and bats to all of the students as they crowd around him. Brian accidentally drops his glove near my feet. I bend down, pick it up, and hold it out to him. He silently grabs it from my hand and pulls his baseball cap down over his eyes. He walks quickly away from me toward the outfield.

"So... do you miss the old days?" I asked.

"No," Brian said, laughing. "Not really." He awkwardly leaned against the bar. "There's nothing really to miss."

Another disturbing block of silence passed by. I slowly lifted the glass of Coke to my mouth and drank the last of it. "Did you drive to get here?" I asked.

"Yeah," he said. "Why? Do you need a ride?"

I nodded.

"How far away do you live?"

"You know where Patch Road is?"

"Sure," he said. "You want to go now?" He threw a five dollar bill on the bar.

I stepped outside the tavern and smiled politely at him. I pressed my fingers against my forehead and tried to massage the tension away as I slipped into the front seat of his car.

* * * *

"Thanks for the ride," I said.

"No problem."

I smiled, closed the car door, and watched him drive away. I walked across the front yard and lingered for a moment on the grass. Then I pulled myself up and over the wooden railing of the porch and cautiously leaned my body toward the front entrance of the neighboring studio.

Nothing.

I hurdled back over the porch railing and hopped onto the front sidewalk. I slowly stepped through the side entrance into my apartment, turned the lights on, and locked the door behind me. I turned the lights out and climbed into bed.

I was alone.

For now.

Chapter 8

A sick hamster. A sad, staggering mass of clumpy fur, nipping wearily at a honey-glazed bell of sesame seed mix, its eye glued shut. As I watched Joe stumble about the cage, struggling to do the most basic of things, I found myself relating all too well to him.

* * * *

The bell on the pet shop door rang loudly. I walked over the doorway threshold and climbed up a small, carpeted ramp. I passed a big, furry cat sleeping on a couple of cardboard boxes. The walls were lined with sacks of dog food, plush animal beds, and metal cages.

I rounded a corner and saw a young man standing behind a counter, tallying numbers on a hand-held calculator. He looked up when I approached him.

"Can I help you, Ma'am?"

"Yes," I said. *Ma'am.* "Is the manager around?"

He nodded, set the calculator down, and disappeared. While he was gone, I studied the fine details of a plastic model of a submerged ship in an open cabinet. I admired the pose of a deep sea diver as he emerged from a hole in the ship.

"Sarah."

I looked up and saw Brian standing behind the counter. He was dressed in a starchy white shirt and navy tie.

"Now this is a surprise," he said.

"I forgot to mention last night that I have hamsters," I said, quickly. "I keep feeding them the same stuff from the supermarket. I think they're getting sick of it."

He smiled and started walking down an aisle. "Well all the small mammal mixes are the same, no matter where you get them from. They've all got the same little crosses and squares, the sesame seeds with and without the shell, with salt, without salt... I mean, we've got honey-glazed bars and bells of mix, if you want."

"Uh-huh." Speaking of glaze, I felt my eyes doing just that - glazing over. *Good Lord...* I pictured myself in Brian's place, talking animal feed all day, and I envisioned myself hanging from the pet shop rafters. But then I thought about being around all those sweet animals all day, every day, and taking care of them...

"Vitamin supplements," he said. "Do you give your pets any?"

"No," I said.

"Does their fur look clumpy?"

"A little."

"Then they've got a vitamin deficiency." He pulled a tiny white bottle off a shelf and handed it to me. "Give 'em this stuff. Their fur will be shiny and full in no time."

"The eye of one of them is glued shut. I don't know what's wrong," I said.

"That might be due to crust formation," he said. "A cloth moistened with warm water might help."

"And it's started to stagger."

"Ooh, that's not good," he said, blinking hard. "How long has it been this way?"

"Since the day before yesterday."

"It could be on its way out, Sarah. You should take it to a vet."

"Dying?" I asked, mindlessly pulling packages of fruit and nut mixes off the shelf.

"I don't want to say anything else 'cause I haven't seen it," he said. "But that's been my experience. When they start looking like that, it usually means they've caught something. And sometimes it's hard to nurse them back. Call the Animal Hospital."

"Thank you," I said. I lifted a bowl of seeds tightly wrapped in plastic. I pushed my thumb into it and accidentally punctured it. I swiftly shoved the bowl back on the shelf and hid it with another bowl. It was safe to say that the prognosis I had just received for Joey had thrown me. Just a bit.

Brian walked toward the front counter. I followed behind him. I passed by a cage full of baby gerbils climbing over one another and burrowing underneath the shreds and chips lining the bottom of the cage. I stopped walking and peered through the bars. I smiled down at them, and then turned my head toward a wall full of lavender aquarium tanks filled with fish.

"Sarah?" Brian asked. "Is there something else you wanted to look at?"

113

I walked over to the aquarium tanks and quietly watched the fish swim around. I followed a sunfish into a small coral cave. "Do you need any help here?"

He scratched his head. "You're a real animal lover, aren't you?" He paused for a moment and stared hard at the floor. "Jimmy? Jimmy, come over here, will ya?"

The young man ran over to the counter and jumped behind the register. One thing I knew for sure that I'd enjoy if I ever did work there was teaching young Jimmy how a woman closing in on 20 feels about being called "ma'am."

"Get this, OK?" Brian said to him, pointing to the hamster feed.

Jimmy began punching numbers into the cash register as Brian walked over to the aquarium tanks.

"We could really use another person around here," he confided as soon as I reached him.

"Really?"

"Yeah, yeah," he said, staring hard at the floor again. "I just don't know if we can afford to hire anyone... right now."

"Oh," I said, quietly.

"But things are always changing, Sarah. Can you come back again in a few weeks?"

"Uh-huh. Sure."

"I might have better news for you then," he said, forcing a smile.

"Thanks."

He looked as though he were in deep thought as he walked me back over to the counter. I quietly paid for the hamster seeds and smiled awkwardly at him. I walked out through the chiming front door.

* * * *

"Do you have an appointment?" A woman with hair tied in a bun greeted me at the front desk of the Animal Nursing Hospital. Small, gray patches at her temples were strategically camouflaged by lengthy spirals cascading from the top of her head. I wondered how many years it would be before I would start worrying about trying to not look my real age. I thought about Jimmy, at most maybe three years younger than me, calling me "ma'am." Maybe life was making me look as old and haggard as I'd been feeling since I left Boston? Maybe loneliness and despair were prematurely aging me?

I placed a cardboard box on the counter in front of her. "I have an emergency."

"Oh?" she said. She stood up and put her spectacles on. "What do we have here?"

I opened the box. Joe's breathing was labored as he lay still and flat across the stiff, elevated folds of the box. Looking at him was making me anxious, so I turned my head away and focused instead on a necklace dangling against the woman's chest. I wondered if she bought it herself or if someone had given it to her. I looked down at her left hand to see if she was married, but it was hidden inside the box.

"How long have you had him?" she asked.

"Two and a half years."

"Hmmm..." She lifted her hand out of the box and pressed her long, painted fingernail against a schedule pad. She was unmarried. And I was completely obsessing, for some reason. "Might be able to squeeze you in here." She pursed her lips. "For future reference, we usually only take appointments."

I nodded. I wished I had gone with my gut instinct two and a half years ago and bought a goldfish.

A younger woman in a lab coat stepped out from a back room and approached the secretary. She gave me a smile and set a stack of envelopes down on the front desk.

"Do you have time for one more?" the secretary asked her. "A sick hamster?"

The vet pouted her lips and looked toward the box. "Aw," she said, lifting the hamster up and stroking its fur. "Poor baby. Looks like it has wet tail."

"Will he be OK?" I asked.

She delicately placed Joe back down and gathered some Kleenex from a box on the secretary's desk. "Keep him warm," she said softly, layering the pieces of tissue over the animal. "Give him this every couple of hours," she said. She pulled a medicine dropper out of a small white bottle and lifted the hamster's head up slightly. She fed it some dark, viscous liquid. "Just give him this and we'll see."

* * * *

Joe died sometime in the early evening back at the apartment, after I had fallen asleep. I woke up shortly after midnight to find him huddled in a corner of the cardboard box facing my bed. I had spent several hours holding him in the palm of my hand and feeding him medicine from an eyedropper before I placed him in the opposite corner of the box facing away from me. I wondered if he knew he was dying and was trying to say good-bye.

I forced myself to stand and tossed a used tissue into a bulging trash bag by the refrigerator. I reached for a fresh one near the kitchen sink.

I then heard a clicking sound. Outside. The click of a latch? From next door? It was followed by footsteps. I froze in place with the tissue dangling in my hand and moved slowly away from the French doors. I sat down on my bed and stared at the motionless blinds.

The French doors started to rumble and slowly creaked open. I jumped to my feet and choked on a gust of air that I inhaled too quickly.

Standing under the porch light, in between the open French doors, was a familiar face shaded by a familiar cowboy hat, staring at me with a familiar greasy smile. He walked toward me and placed his hands around mine. He pulled me toward the French doors and out onto the porch. My body dutifully followed his lead like a disciplined soldier, despite both my head and legs feeling heavy and numb.

117

Perhaps it was shock.

Or perhaps it was a white flag of surrender waving helpless and hopeless submission to this relentless and tireless madman.

I was shaking. I was not going to play victim. I jerked away from him and tightly gripped the porch railing, my eyes suddenly laser-like and penetrating.

He stood a short distance away from me in front of the open doors of the neighboring studio. He was smiling widely at me. "You should be a little more careful about keeping your place locked up," he said. He motioned toward the French doors with his hand. "Any lunatic could just walk right in from off the streets."

"Those doors were locked," I said, my voice monotone, yet quavering.

"Yeah, but you left your window open." He grinned devilishly.

I swallowed hard. "What do you want?"

He thrust his hands deep into the pockets of his long, black coat.

"Come on..." I said in a broken voice. "What do you want from me?"

He remained silent.

I tightened my grip on the porch railing and pressed my back into it. "How did you find me?"

He wiped his mouth with the back of his hand. He leaned his shoulder against the brick wall of the building and let out a heavy sigh.

"You're stalking me," I said, stating the obvious. I tried to stop my lower lip from vibrating with my thumb.

"There's a big difference between *stalking* and trying to *talk* to someone who keeps *walking* away!" he yelled.

I squinted my eyes at him. "Talk about what? What do you want?"

He smiled and looked down toward his feet. "You shouldn't have left me the other night."

I stared at him.

"I don't mean to scare you," he said. He reached out to touch my arm.

I pulled away and pressed my body against the porch railing. "Why are you following me?" I asked.

He cocked his head to one side and laughed. "I'm not following you."

"You're not?" I asked. Unless we were in a wormhole, I failed to see how his argument held up.

"This is fate," he said, laughing.

"What are you talking about?"

"What do you think I'm talking about?"

"I have no idea." I glanced up at the sky in a weak attempt to escape the insanity, if only for a second. I watched a string of clouds glide past the hazy glow of the moon.

"Could you look at me when I talk to you?" he asked. He put his forefinger under my chin.

"Who are you?" I asked.

"You know me."

"No, I don't."

"Yes," he said, laughing. "You do."

"I swear I don't."

He threw his hands up in the air. "Clueless..." he said, turning away. "Totally clueless!"

He wiped his mouth and nose with the back of his hand. Limping, he walked back toward me.

"Sarah..." he whispered, grinning mischievously.

"You know my name."

"And you know mine." He hovered over me. He gently wove his fingers between mine, which were trembling. "You do know who I am," he breathed in my ear.

"I... don't..." I shook my head. "I don't..."

"Sarah..." he whispered, smiling inscrutably. "Seems like fishing at Angel Rock Leap was only yesterday, doesn't it?" He lifted his hat off his head.

I gazed at him and searched his face. I suddenly saw a little boy in them, a vague remnant of purity and innocence flashing in his eyes. He bowed his head and placed his hands on the railing behind me. He looked into my eyes for a long time without saying a word.

"Doug?" I said. I was horrified.

He smiled and pushed himself away.

I stood and stared at him in silence. "I don't believe it," I said, swallowing hard. The horror quickly dissipated and an odd fascination took its place. I could just barely make out traces of someone I did at one time actually know. Someone I did at one time... actually love, in the way children love. The weathered skin under his eyes and long, unkempt hair shielded me from recognizing the innocence I had once known. It had up to that moment made it impossible for me to see anything other than the formidable freak my long lost prepubescent sweetheart had obviously morphed into over the years.

"I just can't believe... it's you," I said, shaking my head. "After all these years." I slowly walked past him and peered inside the neighboring studio. There was just a crate and a kerosene lamp in the middle of an otherwise dust bunny-covered hardwood floor.

"So curious," he said. He moved in front of the apartment and lightly pushed me with the back of his fist.

My brain felt like a top spinning inside my head. I had to sit down on the porch.

"How long have you been here?" I asked. I tried hard to catch my breath.

"As long as you've been..." he said. A Cheshire grin slowly formed on his face. He moved close to me and leaned his head down toward mine. He whispered in my ear, "Fate."

"Look at you," I said. "After all this time." I could see him again, even more clearly. The walking and talking embodiment of a memory I'd been cherishing and rehashing for years, alive and breathing right before my eyes.

"Like you really care." The mood instantly changed. Using the brick wall behind me, he pushed himself away. "You didn't even know who I was."

I blinked hard. "You were only a little boy the last time I saw you," I said.

"Well you haven't changed." He lit a cigarette and blew smoke rings over my head. "Haven't changed. Same soft, red hair, falling... down past your shoulders. Cute little glasses. Sweet face."

I leaned my head back against the wall and stared at him.

His palms rested against the porch railing. He fixed his gaze on the stormy night sky. Slowly turning, he said, "Everything was so simple when we were kids." He leaned toward me and smiled.

I watched him smoke his cigarette in silence. I figured that it was only a matter of time before I would be awakened by a cough or a twitch and realize I had only been dreaming.

"How did you find me?" I asked.

He smacked his lips together as he drew off the end of his cigarette. He remained silent.

"Doug?"

"What?"

"Did you hear me?"

"No..."

"I asked you how you found me."

He sighed loudly.

"Doug?"

"What? I found you. How I did it isn't important," he said.

I stared down at my hands and pretended to even out the rough edges of my thumbnail. "OK," I said. "Then *why* did you find me?"

He knelt down and let his hands droop between his bent knees. He watched closely as ashes fell to the wood below him and sparked before dying out. He rested the back of his head against the porch railing and drew a large breath. He let the air slowly escape from his lungs.

"I can use your help," he said, putting the cigarette to his mouth.

"What do you want?"

He broke the rest of his cigarette in half and threw the pieces behind him.

I bent my legs and crossed them in front of me. "What can I do?"

"I'm not sure." He smiled crookedly. "Do you know how crazy I was about you?"

I swallowed. "I just mentioned you the other day to someone," I said. "I still think about you." I reached out to touch his knee, yet I couldn't keep my fingers from shaking.

He placed his hand on mine and squeezed my fingers gently. The sweat from his palm dampened my skin.

"I never forgot you," I said.

Suddenly, he stood up. He let go of my hand. "Go away..." he mumbled.

"What?"

"Go... away."

"What? Why?" I asked.

"Go away!" he yelled. "I'm serious!"

"What's wrong?" I asked.

"Just go." I watched him spit over the porch railing and wipe his mouth with the sleeve of his coat.

I scrambled inside the studio. I closed the French doors and locked them into place. I shut and locked the window and crawled into bed. I had been shaken out of my daze by reality. The Doug I had known years ago was gone.

Replaced.

By someone I did not know.

Someone I did not understand.

I soon heard a soft rapping sound. I buried my head under the blankets and waited for the noise to stop. Yet the rapping continued to grow louder and louder until it turned into pounding.

"I want to go for a walk," I could hear him say through the doors. He had stopped banging.

"I... don't think so."

"Sarah, please let's go for a walk." I listened to him pacing unsteadily back and forth on the porch. "You can do whatever you want," he said. "But I'd really like to go for a walk with you."

I slowly approached the French doors and peered through the blinds. I watched him hurdle over the porch railing and limp across the front lawn. He turned slowly around.

"I'd really like to go for a walk!" he called out to me.

I continued looking at him from behind the door. I slowly unlocked it, and even more slowly opened it. I couldn't explain exactly what I was feeling, but it seemed to be a whole mix of intense emotions bouncing off one another and pushing any remnant of reason far out of the reach of my brain. Suddenly he wasn't just a phlegm-spewing nutcase.

He was...

I looked at his dangling, unwashed hair.

I thought back to his ill-timed, oily grin.

I recalled his recurring presence... at the T stop in Boston, on the train in Boston... and everywhere I seemed to be at any time in New York.

He was... a phlegm-spewing nutcase... that I had known before he became a phlegm-spewing nutcase.

The phlegm-spewing part I could marginally deal with.

The nutcase part I couldn't.

"I'm not going anywhere with you!" I called out to him.

He stared at me, blinking.

I stared intensely back.

"But I want to go for a walk," he said. "With you."

I shook my head in disbelief. "What the hell is wrong with you?" I asked, suddenly, amazed at my own brazenness. Astounded by my directness. Shocked by my fearlessness.

He slowly walked back toward me. "What makes you think there's something wrong with me?"

I laughed. "OK," I said, still chuckling. "My bad. You're fine."

He set his hat back on his head and stared at the grass below his feet. "Sarah," he said.

I was quiet.

"Sarah, I missed you so much. For so long."

I just looked at him. I didn't say anything. I couldn't find words anymore to express what I was feeling. And that was because I honestly didn't know what I was feeling.

"You never wrote me back," he said.

"What?" I asked.

"You never answered my letter," he said.

"What letter? I never got a letter from you."

"I wrote you a letter right after I moved away with my dad," he explained. "You never wrote me and I figured you didn't feel about me the way I felt about you. I mean you never even responded. And we had been so close."

"Doug, I never got any letter."

"I still remember where you used to live," he said. "68 Langely Road."

I shook my head.

"I remember how I felt when I wrote the letter," he continued. "When I wrote your name and address. I was so excited dropping that thing in the mailbox. Hoping so badly it'd reach you. Wanting so much to hear back from you."

"Doug," I said. "We didn't live at 68 Langely Road. We lived at 86 Langely Road."

His face lost its color. "You're friggin' kidding me."

"No," I said. "Not kidding. You must have sent a letter to the wrong address."

He started giggling. The giggling turned to laughter. It was the kind of laughter usually bitterly accompanied by the phrase "Murphy's Law." "I don't friggin' believe it," he said. "I sent the letter to the wrong place."

I nodded, curious about what he had written and wondering how I would have felt if his letter had reached me. I had missed him so much, but never knew exactly to where in New Hampshire he and his father had moved. I never knew, and being clueless and twelve, it had never occurred to me to find out.

"All these years I thought you got the letter, and didn't care enough to write back."

I managed to get myself to give him a half smile. "I always cared. I didn't get the letter." And I found myself at that very moment wondering what would have happened if I had actually received it. Or if maybe we had been just a year or two older and had begun using e-mail. Where would I have been so many years later? Where would he have been? Would we have stayed in touch? And if so, would it have made a difference? Would I still have ended up a failed college student-turned-waitress, standing on the porch of a two-by-nothing studio apartment, only a few blocks away from one of those Super Kmarts with the specialized mobile home parking lot spaces notoriously built in economically-depressed areas? And would he have turned out the way he did? However and whatever that, in actuality, was?

"Sarah," he said. "I..." His voice trailed off. "I... I am so..." He turned his body away from me.

"What, Doug?"

He stared solemnly down at the ground. "I... am... so..." He turned again to face me. He sighed heavily. "Lost."

I instinctively started to reach my hand out toward him then, without at first even realizing what I was doing. He was a distance away, too far away for me to touch anything but air. Yet I discovered myself at that moment actually wanting to touch him, to console him.

"So what the hell was up with your mailman back then? Or your neighbors?" he asked. "Why didn't that letter make it to you?"

I shrugged. "I don't know."

"OK, so I get that I screwed up on the address. But doesn't that kind of stuff happen all the time and letters still make it to where they're supposed to go... eventually?"

"I think so few people write letters these days, even then," I said. "Maybe an anthropologist nabbed it and it's sitting in a glass case in the Smithsonian," I joked.

"Seriously, man," he said. "How much effort does it take to stick a letter back in a mailbox and lift that flag thing up?"

I nodded in agreement. And then it occurred to me. 68 Langely Road. I wasn't positive, but I was fairly sure that was where Pamela's family lived.

"So tired of things going wrong," he said. He threw his hat hard on the ground and swept his hand angrily through the hair covering his forehead. He quickly composed himself and stood quietly, his hands pressed firmly against his hips. "I needed to see you again, Sarah."

"But why..." I said, my eyes wide and pleading. "Why the chase, Doug? What... the hell... is *wrong* with you?"

He rubbed his forehead with the tips of his calloused fingers. "I wasn't sure if you wanted to see me again."

"Not like *this*!" I yelled. "How could you think for a second I would want to see you like this? Are you out of your mind?"

"Pretty much," he said, slowly lowering himself to the ground and taking a seat next to his unfortunate hat. "That can happen when you lose... everything."

I pressed my pelvis into the porch railing, and lethargically dangled my arms over it. He was saying too much that I was relating to. Too much for me to just walk away, even though I knew any sane person would have.

But I, myself, wasn't sane.

I had also felt like I lost... everything.

And with everything had gone my mind.

I hurled my body over the railing and stood on the lawn, looking at him. I slowly made my way over to where he was and took a cautious seat next to him.

"What happened to you, Doug?" I asked, softly.

He sighed and shrugged.

I placed my hand on top of his.

"I didn't mean to scare you," he said, gently taking hold of my hand in return.

"Well, you did," I said, not sure if I should have given him the privilege of being so close to me. But something was pulling me toward him. Some obscure, invisible force that I didn't understand.

My own insanity?

"I found out you were living in Boston," he said. "And I had to see you."

I slipped my hand out from underneath his. "Why didn't you let me know who you were? I don't get all this."

He stood up and took a few steps back from me. "Just... afraid," he said.

"Afraid of what?" I asked.

"Afraid... of losing... again," he said. "But you know what, Sarah?"

"What?"

"I still want to take a walk." He started to move toward the edge of the lawn and out toward the street. "I would love your company, but if you don't want to go, I'm going by myself."

As I watched him move further away from me, that mysterious force began tugging at me again. I moved mechanically toward the cold night air.

Toward him.

I followed closely behind as he led the way. It didn't take long before I realized where he was taking me. He held his hand out when we reached the dirt trail leading to the ravine. He gently pulled me into the thicket.

He lit a cigarette when we reached the water and stood, staring into the woods. He stepped onto a rock and took a seat. He flicked some cigarette ashes onto the limestone beneath him and looked at me.

"I've been seeing too much of this place, lately," I said.

"How could you see too much of *this* place? It's beautiful here."

"No, no... It is. You're right," I said. I sat on the flattened rock across from him. "It's just that it... makes me kind of sad."

He blew a swirl of smoke into my face. "We met here. What are you saying?"

I shook my head. "Nothing."

"Talk to me," he said, slowly, a hint of irritation in his voice. He started coughing loudly into his fist and then spit forcefully over the rock's edge.

I sighed. "What happened before?"

"When?" he asked.

"Back at the apartment. What happened?"

He remained quiet. He simply continued to smoke, as if I didn't say anything. I picked up some pebbles and casually tossed them back and forth in my hands.

"I saw you with Pamela," he said, suddenly breaking the silence.

I looked up at him curiously. "You know Pamela?" I asked.

"I saw you with her at the Willow Branch," he said.

"You were there? The other night?"

"Yeah."

I softly bit the insides of my cheeks and studied his face. "I didn't see you."

"I didn't go in," he said.

I looked at him uncomfortably. "It's kind of amazing, you know?"

"What is?"

"The way you seem to be anywhere you want to be at any time... finding out anything you want to know about... anyone."

"It's not so amazing." He laughed and flicked some ashes into the water.

I glared at him. "I don't like being followed."

He smiled.

I listened to the sound of leaves rustling in the autumn breeze and watched the silhouettes of bats flying over a stretch of nearby trees.

"You really sorry I found you?" he asked.

I quietly rocked back and forth with my hands resting on bent knees.

"It's not like we don't know each other," he whispered, as if letting me in on a secret. He swept his fingers through his long, tangled hair and stared up at the sky.

"You don't know me," I said.

He drew hard on his cigarette and let the smoke come out through his nostrils in narrow streams. "But we both know Pamela."

"Why do you keep saying her name? How do you know her?" I asked.

He took a deep breath of crisp air and exhaled slowly. "You get to know someone really well when you live with them."

My eyes locked into place and stayed fixed on his shadowy outline. It was a strain to keep my eyelids raised, yet I refused to blink for fear of missing something. "You're not..." I said, unable to finish my sentence. "Wait a second. I don't fol-..."

"Follow what?" he interrupted, with that strange, seemingly untimely smile of his creeping across his face.

"Did you... I can't..." I stuttered.

He looked at me, quiet. He swept his hand across his mouth and continued to look at me. There was a hint of pain in his eyes, the strange smile still cradling his nose.

"Were you the one who..." My voice disappeared behind an unexpected gasp.

He said nothing. He just sat very still. He finally stood up and, towering over me, said barely above a whisper, "She ruined my life." He grabbed a fistful of stringy hair hanging in front of his forehead.

"What happened?" I asked.

"Why can't we see what's coming?" He bent down, cupped a pool of water with his hands, and threw it at his face. "Why can't we just jump out of its way?"

"I don't understand," I said. "What did she do to you?"

He sighed and moved his hands over his face. He then raked his fingers through his hair. "Don't get it." He lifted a piece of shale and threw it hard into the trees on the other side of the water. "Just don't get it." He picked up another rock and threw it into the same space the first stone was aimed at. He looked at me briefly. He then picked up a third rock twice the size of the other two. "You know I was on a football scholarship? I was a cornerback. On defense." He shifted his weight to his back leg and drove the last rock hard into the woods. A cloud of bats lifted up and out of the trees and flew over our heads to a safer part of the surrounding forest. "I came back here, a football player so good at what I did they paid me for it."

"Is that where you and Pamela got together? In college?"

He pressed his lips to his cigarette and then moved it away from his mouth without inhaling the smoke. "I used to watch her. I watched her every chance I could get. All that grace, and strength... All that energy." He pinched the end of his cigarette butt and tossed it into the water. "She taught me how to walk on my hands..." He stared down at his feet and kicked some dirt and pebbles out from underneath his shoes. "She taught me how not to walk on my legs."

"What?" I asked.

He continued to look at the ground and roll small siltstones back and forth with the soles of his shoes.

"What do you mean?" I asked.

A bat fluttered over our heads and landed in a nearby tree. Two more followed closely behind it, taking the time to soar gracefully in wide circles in front of the moonlit sky.

"What?" I asked. "What happened?"

He looked down at his feet. He slowly nodded, almost as if he were having a conversation with himself in his mind. He placed his hand underneath his shirt and started to slowly scratch his chest. "She ruined my life."

"How so?" I asked.

"Huh?" He stared at me and squinted his eyes as if he were trying to bring his mind back from a distant place.

"I'm just trying to understand what went on between you," I said.

He looked at me vacantly. His fingers slipped under his shirt and he began massaging his bare, protruding stomach.

"How did she ruin your life?" I asked, pointedly.

He wrinkled his forehead. Even though he was looking into my eyes, I could tell that he didn't really see me.

"I got home late one night," he said, distantly. "Got to the front door. Guess she heard me because she opened it. Either, that, or she was just waiting there for me. Waiting to shove me down the stairs in the front of the apartment. *Two flights.*"

I stared at him in silence.

"It ripped apart the cartilage in my knee," he said, softly. "Tore my ACL."

"ACL?" I asked.

"Anterior... cruciate... ligament," he said, making sure to enunciate each word. His voice quavered. "I had to quit everything I started." He shifted his gaze from my eyes to my mouth.

"Were you ever violent toward her?" I asked.

"Never," he said. His eyes were wide and penetrating. "*Never.*"

It grew quiet. The silence was interrupted only by the sound of wind snaking through trees and skimming the surface of the water. I looked away from his face and squinted toward the cloudy night sky in search of more bats. I thought I could see a black form partially hidden between a couple of elevated branches, yet it was just a shadow from the tree.

"I'm sorry," I said.

He shrugged and continued to rub his stomach. "There was a time when she looked up to me. She came to all my games." He groaned and tugged hard on the end of his shirt. "Then... things changed."

"How long were you together?"

"I took that football scholarship," he said, ignoring my question. "I came back here, hoping that I'd... see *you* again. I asked around, mentioned your name. I was told you had moved away."

My eyes widened. I looked at him. "I... kind of ran away from here," I said. "Couldn't stand the thought of hanging around. I don't even have family here anymore."

"But you're back here now," he said.

I nodded.

He started laughing and shaking his head in disbelief. "That Pamela. We ran into each other one day on campus, and she was flirting like crazy... Came after me, just the same as she used to when we were kids."

"She did?" I asked. "She used to flirt with you when we were kids? I don't remember that. I didn't even know you knew her back then."

"Yeah, well, I knew her," he said. "But I only had eyes for you." He drew from his cigarette. "I knew even back then that you were the love of my life."

I turn my face to look at Doug and I smile. He smiles back, his curly brown hair falling in front of his eyes and partially shading their gleam. He kisses my cheek and helps me reel the fish in.

I hear a rustling noise in the nearby woods. I figure it is probably an animal scurrying about and rummaging for food. I turn my head in the direction of the sound, and I am surprised to see a person standing in the brush. Whoever is there is too far away for me to really see.

"I don't think we're alone," I whisper in Doug's ear. I quietly gesture with my thumb.

He looks quizzically over his shoulder, a sly grin suddenly forming on his face. "Yeah, it's no one. No one you need to worry about." He kisses me softly again on the cheek.

I stood up and broke some twigs into smaller pieces. I tossed them into the water surrounding us. Tiny ripples splintered the reflection of the moon into many fragments.

"Say something," Doug said. A heavy rock was tossed from behind me, creating thunderous waves, splashes, and ripples. The glowing lunar image on the water was again shattered.

"I guess I don't really understand how you could get involved with someone like her," I said.

"Yeah, right. How could I? How could I be so stupid? Huh? What a loser I am." He started pacing frantically back and forth on the rock.

"Come on," I said. "Calm down."

He didn't listen. He continued quickly pacing back and forth. He started tugging hard at the hair dangling over his eyes.

"Doug..."

He slowed down and folded his arms across his chest. He stood very still in the center of the rock and stared down at his feet. He pulled another cigarette out and slapped his hands against his pockets. "You got a match?"

"No."

"I need a smoke." He nervously paced back and forth on the rock. He then walked toward a pile of ashes and smoky branches from a fire that had been lit earlier. He bent down and picked up a discarded book of matches. He lit the tobacco and knelt down in front of me, blowing a thick, choking cloud of smoke into the air.

I cleared my throat. "You said you needed my help with something?"

"I changed my mind," he said.

"Come on." I rested my hand on his shoulder. "What did you want?"

He cupped my face in his hands. "You can't help me. My life is over." His eyes were glossy and bloodshot.

"Doug..."

He looked at me for a long time. He drew on the end of his cigarette and sighed heavily. "I was hoping... that seeing you again would help me."

"Has it?" I asked.

He started coughing. He spit into the nearby water. "I don't think there's anyone... or anything that can help me," he said. He spit again into the ravine.

I searched the rock for a dry surface to rest on. "Don't be that way," I said. "Don't think that way."

"Think?" He split his cigarette into two pieces and threw them toward his shoes. He then began smashing them into the rock with his foot. "I stopped thinking a long time ago." He pressed his foot one last time against his cigarette butt. "Did you know..." he said, lighting another cigarette and drawing hard on its end. "Did you know that there's no other person who's ever made me feel the way you did?" He scratched his chest.

At that moment, I could barely hear him. I tried to look into his eyes, but no matter how hard I tried I couldn't see his face. I was too consumed by my thoughts. Too lost in my emotions.

He pinched the end of his new cigarette and spread its ashes across the rock. "You haven't changed," he said. "You have no idea how much I love that hair," he said, reaching out to lift a lock of it. "Friendly eyes. Freckles." He smiled. "Purity." He stared thoughtfully down at the rock below him.

I felt droplets of cold water strike the back of my head, and then my neck. Soon, heavy streams of rain fell from the sky and crashed against the limestone and still water. Doug took his coat off, draped it over his head, and pulled me under it with him. We walked quickly and quietly home together, huddled under our dripping, ready-made umbrella.

We reached the apartment. He hurdled over the railing onto the porch and pulled me up with him. He continued to hold the coat up over both of our heads while he stared down at me, breathing heavily. I let my body lean into his and rested my forehead against his chest. I felt his arms slowly wrap around me and his hand move up the back of my neck to cup my head. A sweet warmth crept through my body as he swept his fingers gently through my hair.

"Innocence," he whispered. He bent down to kiss me lightly on the cheek. "Remember?" He rubbed my chin gently with his thumb.

I felt like a kitten in his arms. I grew sleepier and sleepier with every stroke of his hand through my hair. This wasn't the same person I had been running from. This wasn't the same person I had been so afraid of. He was a window into the only part of my past that I wasn't running from, that I wasn't afraid of. He was the only part of my past that made me feel like life could be everything I wanted and needed it to be.

As we stood together on the porch, the rain slowed to a light trickle and the early dawn sky turned a pale blue. Finally, we drew away from each other. He went to his home, and I went to mine.

I lingered for a moment in my doorway and listened to the crackling sound of the drizzle hitting the ground. It seemed that these sudden heavy rains were out of time, a season or two too late. Yet, like everything else, they were still welcomed with open arms.

Chapter 9

I reached the diner to find Pamela rushing from table to table, her head bent low and her face flushed. There were people seated almost everywhere, clanking their utensils loudly and engaging in loud conversations and laughter. Pamela flew behind the swinging doors of the kitchen and emerged with armfuls of plates filled with steaming food. She looked up briefly when she saw me standing at the front entrance, and placed the plates down in sequence at a table. She ran over to me.

"You're late," she scolded.

"Matt told me to come in at noon."

"The weekdays here are murder! We always need at least two people for the morning shift! What is he... on something?" She briskly walked away from me and stood in the middle of the diner with her hands on her hips. "You get in here at nine o'clock from now on."

"This wasn't my fault," I said in a low tone. I walked swiftly past her toward the kitchen. I threw my coat against a rack in the storage room and watched it fall in a heap on the floor. I grabbed a clean apron from a large cardboard box and furiously wrapped it around my waist. Fumbling with the string, I tried to make a nice bow. Yet out of anger I fashioned a tight knot.

"You've got all the stations," Pamela said. She was sitting at the doorway of the storage room. "I'm going on break."

I tried to loosen the apron string so that I could start over. "When's Matt going to get here?"

"You just missed him. He's on vacation for a week," she said.

I pulled the apron up and over my head and thrust it into her hands. "Here. I'm done." Sheer disgust seemed to have taken hold of my reins and was now steering me.

I started toward the doorway. Pamela grabbed a clump of hair hanging over my forehead. "You're so weak," she hissed, pulling my hair tighter.

I rubbed the top of my head and swung around to face her.

"Pathetic," she said. A tiny ball of saliva flew from her mouth and landed on my lower lip. There was a lengthy pause at that point, during which I figured she might apologize for literally spitting on me. However, I realized that the pause was just so she could catch her breath before giving my hair one final yank and pushing me. Returning the favor, I took a fistful of her cropped, wispy hair and tugged on it as hard as I could. She raised her knee and pressed the bottom of her shoe against my rib cage. Just as I managed to cover her face with my hand and squeeze it with my fingertips, I felt two arms wrap around my waist and pull me away from her. I could smell the underarm sweat of the head cook as he lifted me a few inches off the ground and placed me in the storage room.

"I'm sorry," Pamela said to him. She was breathing hard and smoothing out her dress and apron. Her hands jumped to the tangled, unruly mess on the top of her head, which she quickly tried to mat down with shaky fingers.

"How old are you?" the cook angrily asked her.

I moved closer to her and looked into her icy blue eyes. "Where's it all coming from?" I asked, although I was pretty sure I knew. Things were not going well for her. Hence, things would not go well for those around her. I backed away.

She didn't answer me.

I turned around, walked quickly past the head cook, through the swinging doors, and out the diner exit.

* * * *

The cemetery looked much smaller in the light of day than it did in the dead of night. I walked through the open gate and up the dirt path leading to the tombstones. I knelt down before one, feeling a sudden gust of wind pass over me and hearing it jangle the leaves on some nearby trees. I leaned back and rested my palms against the cold earth behind me.

Family members were on the other side of the cemetery grounds. The inability to battle disease was what led them there. The fight against disease was what also led me to Boston, to the pharmaceutical sciences program, where I would be faced with my own losing battle that led me right back to where I was. But even with all the bouncing around I realized I never lost my desire to make some kind of a difference.

I just didn't quite know how.

A dust and pebble filled gale blew across my face and caused my eyes to blink and tear. It continued for a long while, picking up flowers and tissues and carrying them across the length of the graveyard. I stood up and gently trailed my finger along the length of my scalp, which was still sore. I reached down to pull some scraggly weeds out of the ground and matted the uprooted soil with my fingertips.

Restless, I walked over to a wind-blown bouquet of flowers and picked it up. I dug a small, but deep hole in the ground between two tombstones and crammed the tips of the stems into it. I patted the soil around the flowers and stared at the pretty display of tulips, lilies, and lilacs standing at a tilt in the dirt. A chill passed through me, and I found myself admiring how peaceful and protected the flowers looked with their sturdy stems mashed into the ground.

I turned around and walked back up the path toward the tall, black metal gate. As I passed through it, a blast of cold wind hit me from behind and sent all of my hair flying forward. I turned to face the wind head-on and took one long, lingering look at the cemetery before continuing onward to the world of the living.

Or a variation thereof.

* * * *

I reached my apartment. I flopped my body down on my unmade bed and buried my face in my pillow. I stood up and walked over to the miniature wild brush habitat I had created for the hamster. I saw some partly chewed dried corn and wheat middlings sparsely scattered across his bedding. I realized that it had been several days since I had given him fresh food and water. He stood on his hind legs and stared up at me with mucus-lined eyes and a sulky expression.

I hovered over him and poured capfuls of food into his tank. He eagerly raced over to the piles of soy bean hulls, sunflower seeds, and alfalfa pellets, nudging and pushing pieces of food away with his nose.

The late afternoon sun streaming through the cracks of the French door blinds made me feel anxious, like I was playing hooky from school. I lifted the blankets off the bed and shook them. I heaved a sigh as I solemnly watched a cloud of dust rise up and thicken the stale air in the apartment. I opened my manila folder and pulled out one of my poems.

The lone soldier walks on limbs filled with fatigue and weakness,
dragging his hunched torso toward the nearby security, his home.
His tiny eyes, hidden under strands of long, filthy hair,
spy the grins of demons as they hover about him.
Waters of antipathy coast through the air,
and strike his sensitive skin and trickle south.
His heart dives off its perch and lands silently below,
daring not to scream for fear of response.

His hands remain clenched, tightly gripping the anger
of war,
and he parts from his enemies, he leaves them behind.
Tonight he is isolated, he is safe, he is alone,
but tomorrow he will be in the throes of battle,
once more.

Yep. Uplifting prose from high school, reflecting and reminding me of what I had been through, and what I had felt as I went through it. I folded the poem neatly and placed it in a white business envelope. I signed a cover letter that I had drafted a few days earlier for a literary magazine. I carefully placed it inside the envelope next to the poem. I figured I had put in the effort to capture my darkest moments on paper, to paint my worst memories with words. Now was the time to try to give it some kind of meaning and purpose. Now was the time to try to share it.

I heard a light knock. It was Scott, his elbow resting on the rim of the doorway. He looked somber.

"I wasn't sure if you worked or not today," he said. He squinted his eyes at me.

I left the door ajar. I turned my back to him and motioned for him to leave.

"Sarah, forget what I said the other night, OK? I mean, whatever exactly it was that I said. I can't even remember."

I turned toward him again and stared angrily into his eyes. I lowered my head and watched dust balls get carried through the doorway by the wind.

147

"Sarah, you really do mean a lot to me."

I walked away from him. "You mean a lot to me, too."

"So? What's the problem here?"

I shrugged. "You're kind of a schmuck."

"Hey," he said, defensively. "You asked me... No, you *pressured* me for an opinion." He walked over to the French doors and peered out the cracks of the hanging blinds.

"We're the closest of friends," I said. "We're supposed to be comfortable around each other. Able to say and ask pretty much anything we want."

"Sarah, that's just it. We're *friends*. Why all of a sudden are you asking me to look at you like you're a *woman*?"

"I don't know," I said, knowing full well that I was a handful. A needy handful. So needy that even being the proud owner of my own psychotic, obsessive stalker was not enough proof that I was wanted. Although perhaps if the words "psychotic" and "obsessive" were removed from that equation I'd have a better shot at believing. "I guess I was looking for reassurance."

"I can't give you that kind of reassurance," he said. One corner of his mouth was turned up so that his smile looked crooked, almost evil. "Not without feeling like it's going to lead to something I don't want."

"All I asked was a simple question," I growled.

"A loaded question."

148

"You're shallow." I sat down on my bed and clasped my hands. I rested them on my lap.

"Let's knock it off, OK?" he said, pacing. "This is getting really stupid."

I reached for the fringes of the afghan and twisted them around my fingers. "Could you just leave?" I asked.

"What's *wrong*? I really don't understand what's going on with you."

"Please go?"

He threw his hands up in the air and let them drop loudly to his thighs.

"Go," I said, pointing toward the door.

He swept past me, dramatically stirring up a current of stagnant air. "*What do you think of me?*" he mockingly asked Larry as he walked past the hamster's cage. "*As a woman?*" He opened the door and turned around to face me. "Where's the other guy?"

I remained quiet.

"Dead? Escaped? What?"

"You're shallow," I said. "Selfish, one-dimensional, superficial, plastic, balloon-headed, egocentric..." I took a breath. "Narcissistic..."

"I thought I was just shallow," he said. "Don't confuse me."

"Just go, will you?"

He turned the doorknob back and forth. "I'm getting a dull ache between my eyes. It must be all this *closeness* and *comfort* you stirred up between us."

I stared down at the floor with my arms crossed over my chest. I listened to the lonely sound of the door closing behind him. I opened the French doors, walked outside and sat down on the dusty wooden planks. I leaned my back against the brick wall of the building.

I sat motionless for a long while with my eyes tightly shut and my head tilted back slightly, resting. Apart from hearing an occasional car drive by, or the howling protests of a chained neighborhood dog, I felt very removed from everything.

"Sleeping in broad daylight?"

I was jolted by the sound of a familiar deep, hoarse voice. I opened my teary eyes to see Doug's head squeezed between two columns holding up the porch railing. I rubbed the tears away from my eyes and caught glimpses of his oily face and hair. He looked a little more ominous in the daytime than he had in the dark. And yet, knowing who he actually was, helped to put all of his disgustingness in a different context.

"I gotta ask you something," he said. He climbed onto the porch.

"What?"

He pulled out a cigarette from a pack in his coat pocket and lit it. "Could I stay with you for a while?"

My eyes roamed all over the porch while I tried to think of an answer.

"I don't have anywhere to go," he said.

I pointed to the neighboring studio.

"I broke in there, Sarah," he said, as though I should have instinctively known that. "It's only a matter of time before someone finds out."

"I just quit my job this afternoon," I said.

"What does that have to do with me getting a piece of floor to sleep on?" he asked. He was the king of catching me at a really bad moment and asking for attention that I didn't have or want to give.

"I guess it doesn't have anything to do with it," I said. I envisioned the two of us singing ballads over a conga drum in a New Paltz bus station and collecting peoples' pocket change for sheer survival.

He pounded his fist on the porch railing. "You just don't want me around." He dropped his arms over the railing and hung his head down.

I stood up slowly, stretched my legs, and looked at him. "I want you around, Doug," I said, exasperated. "I'm just going through a hard time right now." I motioned for him to come inside my apartment.

He bounded through the open French doors a few minutes later with a shabby, brown duffel bag.

"That's it?" I asked. "Do you have... soap? Shampoo? Towels? Razors? Shaving cream? Toothpaste?"

He gave me an annoyed look. He unzipped the bag and pulled out a tiny slab of used soap, a ripped, frayed washcloth, and a worn-out, soft-bristled toothbrush. "I *just* ran out of the other stuff." I assumed he was one of those types for whom growing a beard was a challenge, otherwise surely by now he would have looked like a member of ZZ Top.

"What have you been sleeping on?"

He ignored me and tossed his toothbrush into the kitchen sink. He walked into the bathroom and peed with the door open. When he was finished, he poked his head out of the doorway. "You got an extra key?"

I was quiet. I smiled at the irony of his sudden civility. It hadn't been a full 24 hours since he thought nothing of breaking into the place. I was tempted to suggest he just use my window as he did in the past. "Is there any way we can share just one?"

"I didn't know we were running on the same schedule."

"I thought you just needed a place to stay for a few days."

He flushed the toilet and spit into the spinning water. I didn't understand what it was with the spitting all the time, but I just let him do his thing and kept silent. He stood very still and stared at me with his hands hiding in his coat pockets. He turned briefly to face the porch and squinted at the blinding sun that was disappearing behind the mountains. "Can I just have an extra key?"

I slowly nodded and lifted one out of my handbag. I laid it down in the sweaty palm of his hand and watched as it disappeared in his fist.

"I need a shower," he said.

Yes, badly, I thought. "Help yourself."

"Hey, what's this?" he asked, emerging from the bathroom after cleansing himself, one of my full-length towels wrapped around his waist and a hand towel around his neck. He walked over to my nightstand and lifted my manila folder up.

"It's my writing," I said, calmly but firmly taking it out of his hands. I couldn't help but stare at his face, cleansed and beaming. He had grown to be strikingly handsome, with his towering height, his wet hair slicked back and not hiding his beautiful eyes, hazel with specks of amber. I noticed he had the same amazingly long and luscious lashes I remembered him having as a child. The transformation a little water and soap could make was beyond astounding.

"What, is it personal or something?" he asked.

I paused. "Yeah, some of it."

He smiled. "I still want to get to know you," he said. "Again. After all these years."

I felt a weirdness suddenly creep and scratch below the surface of my skin. It was like a post-traumatic stress syndrome kind of reaction, I supposed. The words 'I still want to get to know you' were haunting, far too reminiscent of the dodgy cretin I thought I was dealing with not more than a day earlier. His brokenness continued to make me chary, questioning how close I wanted to get to him... how close I *should* get to him.

He drew nearer to me, and slowly reached his hand out toward the folder. He raised his eyebrows at me. "Can you share some of it? Please?"

I hesitated.

"Please?" he asked again, his hand still outstretched.

I slapped the folder a few times against the palm of my hand and stared at him, teasingly. "This holds some of my deepest, darkest secrets."

He grinned. "It's polite to share," he said, softly.

I sat down on my bed, leaned back against the headboard, and slowly opened the folder.

"Funny you have that stuff printed out," he said. "Who does that anymore? Everything's on the *computer*."

I lifted the first loose page I came across and held it out to him. "I think I'm stuck in a different era than most people," I said. "I like having something I can physically hold."

He took the paper from my hand.

"You can read it." I pointed with my chin to the paper he was holding. "Out loud."

"OK," he mumbled, smoothing the crumpled paper out against his hip. "Not long after I learned of my father's... passing..." His voice trailed off. "Your dad died?" he asked.

I nodded, slowly.

"Sorry, Sarah," he said. "I remember your mom was sick..."

"She's gone, too," I said.

He stared at me. For a long time. Without saying anything.

"You want to continue reading?" I asked, finally.

He looked down and hung his head. "Sure," he mumbled, trailing his bare, moistened foot back and forth across the floor a few times. He lifted the paper up again and said, "Not long after I learned of my father's passing, I had received a number of messages from people who knew him, expressing their condolences. While anyone who knew my father was amazed by the incredible person that he was, I think in retrospect it was easy to take him a bit for granted. Because he was always there. Always there to have an in-depth conversation with. Always there to share a meal with. I thought I would see my father again. And have that in-depth conversation. And enjoy a wonderful meal. I took for granted that my father would always be there. How very fortunate I am that my father had such a strong presence in my life. Much love to him, for all that he was and all that he continues to be in a very special place in my heart. He will be there forever." He looked at me, staring again without saying anything.

My eyes were misty. "My mom's eulogy is in there, too," I said, lifting another page out of the folder. I started reading. "My memory grows a little dimmer with each passing day. There were some recent years that passed silently between us." I looked up at him. "That's when she was sick, in the hospital. When you were still living here with your dad."

He nodded. "I remember."

I continued. "But those years were preceded by so many more that I can only describe as vibrant. *Those* are the years that I remember well, and *those* are the years that mean the world to me. We shared so much as mother and daughter. We shared so much as friends." I paused. "Anybody can be a mother. Anybody can be a friend. Not everybody can be both. But you were to me, and for this I am grateful. I will miss you, Mom." I placed the paper back in the folder, and gently pried the page Doug was holding out of his hand. I closed the folder and lay my head back against my pillow, my hand resting on my forehead.

"Those are beautiful," Doug said.

I didn't hear him. "My father drank too much," I offered, suddenly. "He couldn't cope."

Doug's eyes shot down toward the floor. He placed his hand over his mouth and began slowly nodding.

"I have something I wrote about that. I'm thinking about calling it 'Drowning in Sorrow.'"

He looked up at me.

"But 'Riptide' might be more fitting," I said.

He grabbed a chair then and sat statuesque in it, his eyes fixated on me. His hands were clasped together and resting on his large inflating and deflating stomach. He looked as placid as a lake as he sat there, unblinking and staring at me. "*I* could give you some more material," he said, finally. "I wound up in the hospital a few months ago."

I lifted my hand off of my forehead and let it linger in the air, wishing he were a little closer so I could put it on his shoulder or arm or something to let him know I was there for him. But the conversation was draining me. I was listless. Exhausted.

Spent.

"It got to the point where I *had* to drink or I'd get sick," he continued.

I blinked hard. "I can't imagine what it was like for my father," I said. "My mother was his world."

"Well my world was pretty badly shaken up, too," he said, his voice quivering.

"He had the rest of his life," I said. "But he just couldn't see it."

"Or he had the rest of his life, but he just didn't want it," Doug said.

I looked at him. His face for a second had transformed into my father's. "Because he couldn't see clearly enough," I said. "He was blinded by the one thing he didn't have."

Doug sat down next to me on the bed. He lifted my hand up and held it in his own.

"I wish I could have saved her," I said. "That's what inspired me to go to Boston, to college... to that godforsaken career path I chose. But I also wish I could have saved him... from *himself*."

I put my arm around Doug's neck then and pulled him close to me, hugging him tightly. I gently rubbed his back, still moist from the shower.

I slowly drew away from him. I was feeling too much. At least at that moment. And we were too close. I needed some distance. Still keeping my hand on his forearm, I asked, slowly and gently, "So how's *your* dad doing?"

He shrugged. "Your guess is as good as mine," he said.

"You're not in touch with him?"

"Nope."

"Why not?" I asked.

He shrugged again. "Again, your guess is as good as mine."

I touched the side of his face. "Where is he?"

"Maine," he said. "He's working up there now. I haven't talked to him since I told him I was dropping out of school." He stood up.

I rolled over onto my side and clutched my pillow. "He was upset about that?" I asked.

"I guess," he said. "He told me if I quit, I was on my own. So here I am." He started to dry his hair with the hand towel. "On my own."

I stared at him thoughtfully. "Did he offer to support you, so long as you stayed in school?"

He rubbed his head vigorously with the hand towel and then tossed the towel on the kitchen counter. He grabbed a glass from the cabinet and filled it with water from the sink.

"Doug?" I asked, ready to repeat myself. I noticed he had an occasional habit of not answering me. Or at least not answering questions he didn't want to be asked.

"What?"

"I asked you if your dad had offered to support you, if you didn't quit college."

158

He drank the water in thirsty gulps, and then set the glass down behind him. "Yeah," he said. "He offered."

"Why didn't you accept?" I asked. "I mean, you wouldn't be going through what you're going through if you just…" My voice trailed off.

He swept his fingers through his damp hair and clamped his hands around the back of his head. "Didn't want to," he said, plainly. "Look, I'm wiped out. I need to take a nap."

"OK," I said. "OK."

Doug slept soundly on a bouncy foam futon that I pulled out from the back of the closet. It was only early evening, yet he lay motionless. I bent down near him and lightly stroked his head, watching his closed eyelids move about like he was dreaming.

I stared down at the freshly cleaned, wavy locks and ringlets that fell to both sides of his head as he slept. With the grime washed away from his body and hair he really did look like a different person, more like just an older version of the charming little boy I remembered. He slept shirtless on his back, a burgundy sheet twisted around his hips and thighs. I gently touched his chest, caressing the soft brown hairs that covered it. My fingers slipped down toward his beer-bloated stomach, trailing the surface of his bulbous navel. I slowly lowered my cheek to where my hand rested, and I listened to the soothing sound of his breathing.

He suddenly swung his arm up and knocked my jaw with his elbow. He moaned loudly and turned over onto his stomach, grasping the sides of the futon and squirming under the sheet. I rubbed my mouth and moved away from him, listening to his groans gradually wane and turn into snoring.

I grabbed a thick sweater that was hanging on my bedpost and quietly walked outside. Despite the bitter cold and a strong urge to curl up under a blanket, I didn't want to go to sleep. I just knew I would be unable to. I turned to look back at the apartment before I stepped into the car.

It was hard to say what I was feeling.

I drove aimlessly for a long time, finally pulling up in front of the Willow Branch. I felt my body stiffen as I walked through the doorway, immediately relaxing when I didn't see Pamela.

I ordered a soda and took my drink to a dark corner table. I slowly sipped and listened to the sound of some patrons' voices as they joked and laughed. A pang of sadness shot through me.

I lifted my glass to my mouth. I lowered it again, leaned my elbow on the table and felt the surface rock. My drink spilled over, landing in my lap. The table clanked loudly as it rocked back and forth several times. After the teetering stopped, I heard the voices in the room grow quiet and saw three men turn in unison toward me. I forced a smile and lifted my empty glass up for them to see.

"I'll get you another one," the bartender said. "Why don't you move to another table?"

I stood up and looked around the barroom for another dark, secluded place to sit. I saw the front door fly open and Gary stroll in, clad in a heavy down jacket with the collar pointed up. His head was bent down. He walked swiftly past the three patrons and took a seat at the far end of the bar.

"Mike!" he called to the bartender. "What do you have for me to try tonight?"

"Oh, I don't think you're gonna go for this, Gar."

"What is it?"

"It's a smoked ale. Tastes kind of like you're drinking a forest fire."

"Let me give it a shot."

The bartender motioned for Gary to wait a moment while he carried a full glass of Coke over to where I was standing. Gary turned to catch a glimpse of me and then quickly averted his glance.

I carried my glass over to the empty bar stool next to him. I couldn't help but notice that he was physically avoiding looking at me. He lifted a tiny shot glass filled with a beer sample to his lips and drank some.

"Pretty gross," he commented after gulping and wincing.

The bartender smiled. "You want light beer on draft?"

"Nah, give me the bottle, for a change."

I sat quietly next to him, taking small sips and feeling very much out of place. He drummed his fingers on the counter and stared down at his shot glass.

"Hello, Sarah," he mumbled.

I cleared my throat. "Do you realize how long I've been sitting here?"

He turned his head to look at me. "I'm a little slow tonight. You'll have to forgive me."

I quietly nodded and took a sip of Coke.

"So what are you doing back in town?" he asked.

"So far, not much."

"Are you planning on staying here long?" He lifted a bottle of beer that was set down in front of him and tilted it against his lips.

"I don't know."

"There's absolutely nothing going on here," he said. He snickered and wiped his nose with the back of his hand. "I'm really surprised to see you back. Where were you at before?" he asked.

"Boston."

"Boston!" He took a large swallow of his beer. "Why would you give up *Boston* to come back here?"

I sighed. *Why does everybody ask me that?* I let my lips linger for a moment on the edge of my glass. "If you think Boston's so great, why aren't *you* out there?"

He scratched the back of his head. "I'm helping my father out with the business.

I turned on my bar stool to fully face him. "Gary?"

"What?"

"Can I ask you something?"

He shrugged. "What?"

"What did you see in Pamela?" I asked.

He gave me a confused look. "What *did* I see in her? What do you mean *did*?"

"I thought you broke it off with her."

"I still love her," he said.

I looked down at my drink. I slowly looked back up again at his face. "I don't understand."

"What?"

"You always used to tell me how much you couldn't stand her."

He laughed. He took another gulp of beer. "Now how long ago are we talking?" He gave me an irritated look and raised the neck of his beer bottle to his mouth.

I stared at his jaw line, watching closely as a long bone emerged and disappeared behind his skin as he sipped. I examined the tiny black hairs on his cheeks and chin and the way his feathery dark hair curled up against the back of his neck.

"Mike!" Gary yelled. "Two more?" He tilted his bottle and let the backwash flow into his mouth. He stood up and walked over to a wooden table.

I clicked my tongue. "Thanks. I don't like beer."

"Then don't drink it. More for me." He watched the bartender set two beers on the table.

I walked over to where he sat and pounded my fist on the table. "We haven't seen each other in a long time. You can barely look me in the eye."

"Shhh.... Keep your voice down," he whispered.

"Can you tell me what your problem is?" I asked.

"I don't have a problem."

Against my nature, I drank some beer and slammed the bottle down. I stared hard at its neck and clenched my fists. It was too quiet.

"Why are you so angry?" he asked.

"Why are you so distant?"

He pinched the bridge of his nose. He sighed. "You bring me back to a time that I'd like to forget, OK?"

I peeled off the label on my beer bottle and looked up at him. "It wasn't exactly a hoot for me either, Gary."

"I suppose," he mumbled. "But it was much worse for me."

I rolled the label into a narrow cylinder and placed it into an ashtray containing a wad of pink, chewed gum. "What's up with you?"

"Not going to get into it," he said.

I lifted the rolled beer label out of the ashtray again and noticed that the gum was sticking to it. "It seems like nothing's changed since the last time I saw you," I said. I threw the label back down in disgust.

His cheeks turned red.

"What is it?" I asked.

"Pam... I mean, Sarah?" He stared deeply into my eyes.

"What?" I asked.

He looked away from me. He shifted in his chair and started lightly kicking the brass foot rail beneath him. "I just don't feel... what I should... what others seem to..."

I looked down at the table. I wasn't sure what he was trying to say.

"I just don't have feelings I think I should..." he said. "Toward... well... toward anyone, really. And I don't know why."

I raised my head, expecting more. But he had stopped talking. Was he trying to tell me he was asexual?

He slowly stood up. "That's it." He gulped his beer down until his bottle was empty. "I'm gonna get going, all right?" He set his bottle onto the table and walked over to the bar.

"Hey, Mike?" he yelled.

"Yo!" the bartender called back. He pushed himself away from the cash register and walked over to Gary.

"Could you do me a favor?"

"Sure," the bartender said.

Gary reached into the pocket of his jacket and pulled out a small, yellow box decorated with a maroon ribbon. "When you see Pamela, could you give this to her?"

The bartender stared down at the box. "Why can't you give it to her?"

"Because she won't talk to me."

165

"Sorry to hear that," the bartender said. He took the box and shoved it onto a shelf behind the counter. "I'll give it to her. No problem."

"Thanks," Gary said. He slapped some dollar bills onto the counter. He glanced over at me, turned away, and walked out of the tavern.

* * * *

I had been sitting for hours in my bed. I kept one eye on a paperback novel and the other eye glued to the clock by the bedside. It was ten o'clock at night and Doug still had not returned from wherever he had apparently left to go.

I closed my book and threw it carelessly down on the floor in a soft clump of dust bunnies. I turned the light out, hoping to hear the sound of a key turning a lock. Yet all that followed the darkness was the same silence I listened to every night before I fell asleep. I leaned my head against my pillow and tried closing my eyes.

Chapter 10

I awoke early the following morning. A little too early. My eyes were open before my brain was actively firing. I looked over at the base of my bed. The burgundy sheet Doug had been sleeping under was sitting in a rumpled ball on top of the empty foam futon. I stretched my arms over my head, yawned, and slowly sat up. I looked around the quiet, dusty studio and wondered not only where Doug had gone, but where yesterday had gone as well. How did it manage to slip so quickly away from my grasp? I pulled my pillows close to my chest and willed the feeling of emptiness to leave me.

I stood up and sleepily staggered over to the French doors. I peered out the cracks and watched two crows perch themselves on a telephone wire. They seemed to me to be like old friends, standing with their feet tightly wrapped around the thin cord and content passing the time away in each other's company. I climbed back into bed and grabbed my pillows again for comfort.

It is the last time I will see Dawn before we lose touch with one another, although I am not aware of it. She is sitting next to me on a bench facing a huge gray tank crowded with exotic fish circling blue and yellow coral formations. I am mesmerized by the sizes of some of the creatures I see swimming rapidly past the warped, curved glass of the tank and disappearing between the walls of the coral caves. I feel badly that I do not notice at first that Dawn seems sad.

"Is everything OK?" I ask, side glancing a several hundred-pound turtle floating gracefully by.

"Hmmm?" she asks. She picks her head up and forces a smile.

"You seem like something's bothering you." I stare hard into her eyes. I ask, "What's wrong?"

"Eh... I don't know," she says. She clasps her fingers together and pretends to be interested in the tank full of fish.

"What?"

She rolls her eyes. Her lips pout. "Have you ever known me to be happy and in love?" she asks.

I am quiet for a moment. A bright green eel slithering past the window steals my attention. "There was that guy," I say.

"Roy."

"Yeah, Roy," I say. I nod and watch in amazement as a gigantic shark grins its way by, not for a second taking its eye off of me. "Roy."

She snickers. "That only lasted ten months."

I wait in silence for her to continue.

She shifts her position on the bench and moves closer to me. "The guy I'm with now is wonderful. We went to school with him."

"Great," I say, softly. I was half listening, and half really not wanting to hear.

"He'd do anything for me," she says, pressing on despite my obvious lack of attention. "And I know he wants to marry me."

"That sounds nice," I say. I stare wistfully at her. I want her to stop talking. I stand up and motion for her to follow me. She grows quiet.

"So what's wrong?" I ask. I stop in front of a pitch black tank in a darkened hallway.

She leans toward me and whispers, "I still want Roy."

I peer into the tank. I am trying to listen to her, but at the same time I am traveling to the bottom of the ocean as bright green eyes blink at me behind the glass in the surrounding watery darkness.

"Did you hear me?" she asks.

"Yes, I heard." I stare thoughtfully at the ceiling for a moment, trying to convey that I am there. In the moment. With her. But my envy was making me as green as the eyes flashing in the blackness of the simulated ocean floor. And it was making me distant, out of the moment, not with her but instead arm in arm with my loneliness. Hand in hand with my self-pity. And face to face with the fact that I would give anything to have someone love me.

She shrugs. "Every time I'm able to work up the nerve to break up with the guy I'm seeing now, there's some special occasion around the corner that I feel I've got to get through with him," she says. "Like New Year's. Then it's his birthday. The following month is my birthday. Then it's his sister's wedding. Then it's a big party for his parents' anniversary."

"Can't you do it sometime between the special events?" I ask.

She gives me a funny look. "You know that everything's got a lag time attached to it. A week or so before or after a birthday, anniversary, or holiday."

I stare at large black shadows painted on a deep purple wall. They are shaped like whales. I wonder if they are drawn to scale.

Dawn is quiet now. She is quiet and she is staring at the floor.

I start walking away from her, swiftly descending a ramp that is spiraling around the huge, round central tank in the aquarium. Someone in a wet suit with scuba gear and flippers swims by. My eyes are suddenly drawn to the tentacles of a large pink squid pressed against the glass.

"Hey, you want to get going?" Dawn asks.

I am distracted by a candy bar wrapper that is stuck to the bottom of my shoe. Trying to shake it loose from my foot, I say, "OK."

"OK," she says, her voice low and deep.

We start walking together in silence.

My cell phone rang. I reached toward the bedside for it and knocked it off the night table.

"Hello?" I said groggily. I realized I was talking into the wrong end. I turned it around and breathed heavily. "Hello?"

"Is this Sarah?"

"Yes..." I said.

"It's Matt."

I paused.

"I'll try and make this fast, OK?" he said. "My vacation got cut short. And... I heard there was some trouble a couple of days ago between you and Pamela?"

I cleared my throat.

"She told me you quit," he said. "Look, we're really short-staffed. I need you to come in today."

"Well I..."

"We can talk after work if you want to, but for now, I really need you to come in."

"What time does the shift start?" I asked.

"Nine."

"OK..." Groan.

I glanced over at my alarm clock. It was already eight-thirty. I went into the bathroom and turned on the shower. I reached behind me for toilet paper, picked up an empty cardboard roll, and angrily threw it into the shower stall. With my underwear lying at my ankles, I tottered toward the kitchen cabinets and searched for anything soft and absorbent. I grabbed a handful of coffee filters, shoved a toothpaste-covered toothbrush into my mouth, and jumped under a spray of unheated water.

Pamela was bending over and tying her shoe laces when I walked into the diner storage room. She did not look up when I lifted a petite-sized uniform over her head and began undressing. She simply tightened the string of her apron around her tiny waist and stared blankly ahead of herself.

The entire day passed by without her speaking to me or looking at me. With our designated stations, we were fully armed with the perfect reason to have absolutely nothing to do with each other. My only sacrifice was not taking my lunch break, which relieved me from having to share soup and a sandwich in silence in the storage room with her. While she eased herself into a comfortable little crack between heavy sacks of flour and slowly nibbled on a garden salad, I washed down tables with a scowl and a growling stomach.

I decided to stop by the Willow Branch after work to relax. Taking a seat at a table, any chance to kick my heels up flew out the window as soon as I saw Pamela approach the front entrance. She forced the front door open and glared at me. She strutted past some men at the counter. The bartender quickly made his way over to her and pulled Gary's gift out from behind the bar. She smiled down at the tiny package, passed it back and forth between her hands a few times, and then stared icily at me over her shoulder.

"Gary gave this to me to give to you," the bartender said.

"Thanks, honey," she said. She set the gift down on the counter and removed her coat. She was scantily clad, with only a fuzzy mohair sweater that fell to the middle of her rib cage and tight, patched, sixties-styled jeans that embraced her narrow hips. She carefully folded her coat and set it on an empty bar stool. She continued to keep her eyes fixed on me, while the entire bar kept their eyes fixed on her. Finally, she began to slowly unwrap her present.

"A candy sampler..." she said aloud. Her voice was high-pitched. And annoying. At least to me. Smiling widely, she slowly opened the box. She pulled out a tiny chocolate square and bit into it. She stared at me as a string of soft caramel formed between her teeth and the remaining piece of candy.

"Want some?" she asked. She grinned at me and held the box out in front of her.

"Sure," I said. I stood abruptly and then walked over to the bar. I lifted a piece of candy out of the box and looked deep into her eyes. "I'm sure you want *some*, too," I said. I bit into a coconut cream-filled chocolate. "But you're unlikely to get it."

She tossed her head back and laughed loudly. "What are you *talking* about?" she asked. She pulled the candy box away from me.

My heart was pounding. I smiled. "May I have another piece of candy?"

She gave me a strange look.

"Please?" I asked, still smiling.

She threw the box on the bar. "Go ahead... Help yourself to my scraps."

I pooled together the remaining candies and left the box empty. "Pamela." I casually popped an almond-containing chocolate rectangle into my mouth.

"What?" she snarled. She was still pinching the melting chocolate and caramel between her fingers. She took another small, angry bite.

"You are never going to be with Gary the way you want to be with him," I said.

She stopped chewing and stared at me. "How would *you* know *anything* about *anything*?"

"Trust me on this."

She shook her head and looked away from me. "You don't know what you're talking about."

"Ok, keep deluding yourself."

"I'm not deluding myself," she mumbled. She licked some melted chocolate off the end of her thumb.

I smiled demurely. "Yes, you are."

She glared at me.

"Gary is someone who... how do I put this? He's someone who... doesn't enjoy the company of others." I backed away from her and leaned against the bar.

"He... doesn't enjoy the company of others," she parroted. "What the hell does *that* mean?" She held the melted caramel morsel to her lips and looked like she was going to take a bite but then angrily threw it into the empty box. "You know what? I've had enough. I don't know what

kind of trip you're on here, but I have better things to do
with my time than listen to any more of your twisted
babbling." She wiped her chocolate-covered fingers on a
doily she swiped from the bar and grabbed her coat.

"You know..." she said slowly, as she covered her
narrow, bare torso and smoothed down her spiky hair. "It's
funny how all these years have gone by and you're still
burning up inside over *me*."

"I'm sure you wish that was true for Gary," I said,
noticing her eyes starting to tear. I looked away from her
and stared instead at the half-eaten chocolate lying in the
middle of the little box and torn yellow wrapping paper.

I could see a forced grin on her face out of the corner
of my eye. I felt a cold chill run through me as she patted
my shoulder lightly. "I'm so happy to have made such an
impact on you."

I rolled a piece of candy between my fingers and
started to mash it into different shapes. I continued to avoid
looking at her, concentrating instead on the rumpled
wrapping paper on the bar. Pamela drew a deep breath and
exhaled slowly, the air coming out in choppy waves. She
tightened the belt of her coat, threw a couple of dollars
down on the bar, and walked swiftly out.

* * * *

The apartment was dark when I returned. It was after
midnight. I gently turned the key in the lock and silently
crept through the doorway. In a stream of light coming
from an outside street lamp, I could see the hamster in the

aquarium tank standing still on its wheel and an empty foam futon lying at the foot of the bed. The bathroom door was closed and a bright light was shining through the crack where it met the floor. I assumed that Doug must have been in there.

I raced to my dresser. I pulled out a heavy cloth nightgown and slipped into it, half-hoping Doug wouldn't see me before my body was covered. The other half of my hopes was driven by a stabbing, desperate loneliness. I climbed into bed and lay down, trying hard to stay awake. I wanted to see him. Yet I drifted off to sleep not too long after my head hit the pillow.

* * * *

I dozed for a while. I opened my eyes to find the bathroom door open and the light turned off. I lifted my head to see if Doug was sleeping again at the foot of the bed. I saw him kneeling by the bedside, frowning at me.

"Doug... You're awake?" I asked, a bit unnerved at the idea of being watched in my sleep. By someone frowning, nonetheless.

He didn't say anything.

"Doug?"

He sat very still and glared at me.

"What's wrong?" I braced myself for drama.

He slowly stood up and walked over to the window. He leaned his elbow against its frame and stared down at the sidewalk below. I followed his silhouette in the moonlight with my eyes, starting with his bare shoulders and moving to his rounded belly. He was wearing nothing but trunks.

"Doug?"

"What?" he growled. He was still staring out the window.

"Aren't you a little cold?"

He turned to face me. "No."

I sat up in the bed and pulled my blanket up to my chin. "Is everything all right?"

"No," he said.

"What's wrong?"

"Did you go to the Willow Branch tonight?" he asked. "Did you see Pamela there?"

"Why?"

"Just answer," he said.

"Yes."

He paced back and forth. Finally, he sat forcefully down on the futon. He lowered his face in his hands and rocked back and forth, weeping.

I continued to sit upright in the bed, watching him. He cried for a long time. Then he headed for the bathroom to blow his nose in a ball of toilet paper. I heard him kick the base of the toilet. "Ruined my life," he said, blowing hard and then wiping his sore, reddened nostrils. He returned to the futon, threw his drenched toilet paper in the nearby trash, and pulled the burgundy sheet over his head. "But hers goes on."

"Doug?" I whispered.

He lay very still and quiet. Droplets of rain began banging loudly against the window above him. I watched him roll underneath the sheet away from the wall as if trying to shield himself from the noise.

"Doug?"

He gave no response.

"Doug?"

He continued to remain quiet.

"Doug?"

He breathed fast and heavily, but still said nothing. I gently rested my hand on the surface of the sheet. I watched him roll under it to face the pounding rain on the window glass, and I heard him quietly sigh.

"You know, you and I have something in common," I said, softly.

He sighed again.

"We have this... incredible anger."

"What do you have to be angry about?" he grunted. He lifted the sheet off his head and turned to give me a questioning look.

"The same thing you're angry about. I let somebody hurt me," I said. "I let *her* hurt me.

"Pamela?"

I nodded.

He sat up, slowly. "What did she ever do to you?"

I leaned back on the bed. "I don't feel like saying."

"Come on," he groaned.

I pulled the blanket over my knees. "She went out of her way to make me feel like I was nothing," I said.

He laughed. "*That's* all you got on her? We're talking about two different things here," he said. "She ruined my life."

"Doug," I said. "I don't know much about football, but... I have a question for you."

"What?" he asked.

"Realistically," I said, "what were your chances of making it big... if you never got hurt?"

He sat up straighter and started mindlessly folding the edge of the sheet. He stared down at his hands as his fingers sculpted the sheet into a mock fan. "I had won the starting position as cornerback," he said. "I think I had a good chance of being drafted to the NFL."

"What were the chances?" I asked.

"I don't know," he said. "Maybe one in ten?"

"And then if you did get drafted," I said, "what were the chances of you actually making an NFL team?"

He paused, and then slowly lowered the sheet to his lap. The indentations in the sheet he had made quickly disappeared. "I guess maybe one in five? I don't know," he said in a low tone.

"And who's to say you wouldn't have gotten hurt... damaged your knee... in your first game as a pro?" I asked.

"*Look*," he said. "Because of *her* I never even got a chance. She ruined my life."

179

"No," I said. "She made your life *difficult*." I leaned all the way back in bed and pulled the covers to my chin. "*You* ruined your life," I said. "You're *ruining* your life."

There was silence. Only the sound of water smashing against the window and French doors filled the room. I realized I was only partly talking to him. I was mostly talking to myself. It seemed so easy to feel sorry for oneself. And to blame others for a life not fully lived.

We had to have faith. Even if the plan was different from our own, even if we didn't like it. We just had to believe, and follow along.

I leaned toward him. "You can still do so much."

He looked away from me.

"You have the rest of your life," I said, softly.

He slowly lowered his body back on the futon and pulled the sheet back over his head. I could see him turning his body again to face the pouring rain.

Chapter 11

I made a weak fist and knocked on Scott's door. I could see his mother's curlers and ketchup-red hair above the chain through the door crack.

"Sarah?" she asked in her dry, husky smoker's voice. She unhooked the chain with her chubby, freckled hand and opened the door wide, squinting and holding her hand up against the bright sunlight.

"Is Scott awake?" I asked.

"No. He usually gets up around ten or eleven." She rubbed the heavy folds of wrinkled skin below her eyes and yawned.

"Can I see him anyway?"

She looked over her shoulder and toward the bedroom. "I guess so, if it's important." She walked into the kitchen and left me standing alone in the living room.

I lightly knocked on his door and waited for him to answer. I listened to the sound of metal crashing against metal as his mother cleaned out pots and silverware in the sink. I wondered how he could sleep through the noise.

"Scott?" I whispered through the door. I turned the doorknob slowly and stepped inside his dark room.

"Scott?" I whispered again, tiptoeing past the narrow, cranberry-colored sofa he used as a bed. I reached toward a light switch that sat above an old apple juice jar covered with a rubber, eyeless mask. A naked light bulb glowed in the center of the ceiling from underneath hanging stretches of fish net. They dangled only inches away from a life-sized portrait of Sybil Leek guarded in one corner of the room by a semi-circular wooden bar.

"Scott?" I said louder. I poked his shoulder lightly.

"What!" he shouted. He raised his head up off his pillow and let it fall back down.

"Are you awake?" I asked. I poked his shoulder again.

He moaned and pulled his blanket over his head.

"Scott?"

"Whaaat!" He grabbed his pillow and shoved his head under it.

I sat down on a plush cushion near his feet and rested my head on the arm of the couch. I gradually fell asleep.

"Sarah?"

I blinked hard and looked at Scott, sending forth a flood of tears from my tired, itchy eyes.

"How did you get in here?" he asked. He pulled his blanket up to his chin. "I guess a better question is... *why* did you get in here?"

"I'm glad you're awake now."

"What do you mean *now*? You tried to wake me already?"

"Earlier." I reached toward a box of tissues lying at the foot of the sofa and pulled a wad of them out. I wiped my eyes, blew my nose, and rested my head on the arm of the couch again.

"Saaarah..."

"What?"

"What are you doing here?" he asked.

I wiped my nose with a dry, unused piece of tissue. "You don't deserve the way I've been treating you," I mumbled.

"No, I don't," he said.

I drew a deep breath. "I just want you to know that there was no reason for me to get as angry at you as I did."

His tense face relaxed. He leaned against his pillow.

I bent my knees, placed my arms around them, and nuzzled my forehead into the space between my kneecaps. "I just feel like I used to be a better person than I am now."

"In what way?" he asked.

I shrugged. "I don't know... It's hard to put into words."

He nodded.

"There was a time when doing the right thing came so naturally, you know?"

"And now?" he asked.

"And now..." I said, staring down at his blanket. "All of a sudden I'm seeing this whole spectrum of right and wrong that I could fall into at any point in time." I leaned my head back on the arm of the couch. "I always considered myself to be a good person."

"You *are* a good person."

"No. Lately it seems like I'm somewhere in the spectrum I never was before," I said.

"Consider yourself lucky," he said. "I've known people to do things that don't fall anywhere near the spectrum."

"Yeah." I smirked and rolled my eyes. "I'm just filled with so much anger, all the time," I said. I slid off the couch and landed on top of the tissue box. "I'm letting a lot of anger out on a lot of people lately." I stared down at my fingers and pretended to be interested in a hangnail on my thumb. "But you know what? I think the person I'm most angry at is myself."

"There are weeds," he said, "that are treated like roses. No matter how out of control and strangling they are." He paused, lifted up a cup of stagnant water from the floor, and drank it. "Then you have the roses that are treated like weeds. But Sarah?"

"What?"

"Does that mean the roses stop smelling sweet?"

"And I thought *I* was the poet," I said. I stood up, walked to his bedroom door, and lingered near the door knob. I slowly pulled the door open, and then just as slowly closed it again. "Speaking of which, I have some news," I said, suddenly. I handed him a small square piece of paper from the literary magazine I had submitted my poem to. "I'm published, Scott. I have to get this signed by a notary public. And then my work will be in print. Circulation for this magazine is 12,000."

"Holy smokes," he said, holding the paper out in front of himself. "This is so cool. Congratulations, Sarah! So they're publishing a poem of yours?"

"Yes. Thank you," I said. "And I wrote something else, just yesterday."

"You did?" He smiled at me.

"Yes, I did," I said. "I'm trying to channel some of the anger I've been feeling, and do something productive with it."

"You are on a serious roll, Sarah."

"I have it with me, and I'd like to read it to you... if you want."

"By all means," he said, still grinning at me. "I can't wait to hear it."

I took a piece of paper out of my pocket and unfolded it. I cleared my throat. "It's called 'Flatulent Flanagan.'"

His grin broadened. "Sounds like my kind of story."

"There was a gentle breeze that warm, spring day..." I started, "...which tousled my hair, cooled my arms, and made the oversized shorts I was wearing flap against my bony legs. I'd have done anything to be able to have my psyche completely swept up by the hypnotic sweetness of nature that day, as I awkwardly leaned against a tall wire fence near our high school's baseball field and tried to look normal. But I knew I looked anything but normal compared to the others standing nearby, putting my chicken legs and spaghetti arms in awkward positions as I self-consciously struck different poses and tried to make it through another gym class without incident.

"Volleyball with this little group of gangster-types I was assigned to for the semester never had a pretty ending. I had a sneaking suspicion that softball or baseball or whatever our gym teacher had in mind for us that day wouldn't exactly leave me with my toes tapping and a grin on my face.

"Yeah, and so while we were waiting for our gym teacher to return with more gloves or bats or whatever, Latoya Drake started in with me.

"'Hey, you wanna fight?' she asked, glaring at me with squinted brown-black eyes and drawing nearer to where I stood.

"A rhetorical question of sorts. No, of course I didn't want to fight. But like, did I really have a choice?

"She put her fists up.

"I looked away.

"'See my pinky, see my thumb,' she growled, displaying the appropriate appendages, her fists still up in the air and feet dancing around me. 'See my fist you betta run!' She finished the stanza.

"I looked at the ground and kicked some powdery dirt with my feet, knowing at that very moment just how the powdery dirt must have felt, and I silently prayed that our schmuck gym teacher would return from wherever the hell he was. I really hated our gym teacher. Honestly, even if he was there, I knew from past experience that he wouldn't have done anything helpful. Actually, he might have even encouraged Latoya. He seemed to get a perverse pleasure out of rousing the other inmates in this third period penitentiary of Hell and then watching with glee as a prison recreation yard brawl erupted.

"'Let's go!' Latoya yelled, motioning with her two middle fingers for me to hip to the hop and bust a move. 'Scrawny little whatcvuh', she hissed through the large gap between her front, oversized incisors. More Renaissance love poems came flooding forth from her mouth. 'Kick your... What's the mattuh? Didn't eat yo' *Wheaties* today?'

"I had, in fact, eaten cereal for breakfast that morning, but it was either Corn Pops or Froot Loops, so she had me there. OK, so I knew about the fight or flight response, based on an adrenaline rush that helps someone who is being threatened to get out of danger. What I didn't understand was the evolutionary basis for a sudden and unexpected and highly audible burst of gas as you stand there with all these supposedly helpful neurotransmitters coursing through your system.

"Did that really happen?

"No.

"It couldn't have. Did it?

"Oh my.

"Latoya's fists unclenchcd. She looked away from me and shook her head in disbelief. Or was it disgust? Embarrassment? I mean, such a serious, badass affirming moment like what she was striving for had suddenly become an episode of 'Ren and Stimpy.' Man, did *she* pick the wrong nerd to mess with that day.

"As I walked away, I realized something. I had managed to clear not only the air but every living thing that had been within a few feet of me. I was also relieved from fighting this much bigger and more muscular person who could likely pound me with one punch into Middle-earth.

"Could this actually be considered some kind of victory? I wondered as I watched my putz gym teacher return and toss a couple of steel bats and threadbare gloves onto home plate. He lifted a baseball cap off of his bald, sweaty head and looked around at us. A grin swept across his face and he suddenly yelled, 'Let's play ball!'

"I waited to be picked dead last for a team.

"'You're up,' my dumbass gym teacher called to me before handing me a bat. The grin was still on his face, except now it was accompanied by an expectant twinkle in his eye. I wasn't sure how many other gym classes he taught, but I wholeheartedly believed that this was the one he looked forward to the most. He could count on me to fail any athletic challenge he set up, and he could count on my teammates to get really pissed off at me as a result. I sincerely doubted that any of his other classes promised the same level of grade-A entertainment for him as this one did.

"After I struck out, I sat down on a nearby wooden bench and tried to will the minutes away until the bell rang signaling the end of class. *Come on, come on...* I thought, not wanting to spend another second of my time in the company of my dimwit gym teacher or the others or the metal bats or the war-torn gloves.

"I breathed both an internal and external sigh of relief when the bell finally rang and allowed me to get the hell out of there. As I slipped out of my shorts and into jeans in the locker room, I was convinced that the worst was behind me.

"A trip to my locker three periods later convinced me that I was wrong. 'Flatulent Flanagan' was written in block letters with a blue highlighter on yellow-lined paper and scotch-taped to the front of it.

"'Flatulent Flanagan,' was loudly mumbled by a few kids in unison into their fists as they quickly moved past me and my locker and the unassuming yellow piece of paper that was to rapidly become the beginning of the end of my integrity.

"I silently cursed my name and the pathetic ease with which the alliteration had cleverly been developed. I wondered if events like this were random or predetermined, with everything fitting together so perfectly like the pieces of an elaborate puzzle.

"Yeah, so 'Flatulent Flanagan' clung to me like a bad stench throughout the rest of my high school years, and mocked and taunted me right up to the day I graduated. Alas, the moniker 'Flatulent Flanagan' graduated along with me, cloaked in its very own over-sized black gown and sporting a graduate cap with a dangling gold tassel, with honors." I took a deep breath. "That's all I have so far."

Scott paused and stared down at the floor as if he were deep in thought. "That is... so... so... freaking... *awesome!*" he cried, looking up at me and giving me a huge gaping grin. "You're a writer. A writer about gas. One of my favorite subjects!"

"You were my inspiration," I said.

He walked over to me and threw his arms around me, hugging me tightly. "I am so proud of you, Sarah. Seriously."

I melted in his arms. I had found my calling.

Gassy as it was.

Scott suddenly pulled a tiny, wooden staircase down from the ceiling and climbed up into a small, dark attic. "Speaking of writing," he said. "I thought I had those books I told you about in my closet, but I forgot they were up here."

"A room within a room," I said.

"I use this as a retreat so I can get as far as I can away from *her*." He began lowering himself down the ladder. He blew a thick cloud of dust off the top of a small stack of hard cover books and handed them to me.

"These are ghost stories?" I asked.

He nodded.

"You're so... unusual," I said, opening the door a little more and resting my head on it. I sighed and ran my fingers along its rim, picking up a splinter on the way.

He walked over to switch on a lamp. "Are you OK?"

I nodded at him and plucked a sliver of wood from the end of my finger. "Where's your cat?"

"Probably eating trash out of some garbage dumpster." Tying the belt of a terry cloth robe around his waist, he walked into the kitchen, poured some ice cold coffee his mother had brewed into a pan and began heating it on the stove.

"You had to get rid of it?" I asked.

"Yeah, well..."

"Your mother didn't want it?"

"She said if it was a dog, she'd feel differently," he said.

"I can't picture anything more chilling than rolling over on your side and opening your eyes from a sound sleep to find two yellow eyes staring at you in the middle of a ball of jet black fur," I said.

"Picture this..." he said with a yawn. "The same thing happening, except you don't own a cat."

I thought of Doug just then.

I walked into the living room and loitered in the center of its plush, off-white carpeting. I watched as he poured reheated coffee into a mug.

"You want a cup?" he asked from inside the kitchen.

"No," I said. "But thanks."

He walked over to the front door to see me out. The belt of his robe loosened and exposed his flat, hairless stomach and loosely hanging flannel pajama bottoms. "Are you sure you're OK?" he asked. He pulled on his pajamas and let his robe hang freely against his sides.

"I said I was."

He raised his hand, pointed his finger up in the air and opened his mouth as if he were going to say something. He stood frozen solid in the same position for several seconds without saying anything, and finally he whispered, "Are we OK?"

"Why wouldn't we be?" I asked. The chilly early morning air slipped underneath the sleeves of my shirt and made me shiver.

"I guess we've been friends for so long that we can't help but be OK with each other," he said.

I looked away. "We still have to be careful," I said. "Things can happen and things can change."

"Things do happen and things do change," he said, wrapping his robe around himself. He stepped onto the walkway in his bare feet. "I suppose I could be more sensitive."

"Yes," I said, pointing my foot and sweeping my toes across a concrete block in the walkway. "And I suppose I could be a little less sensitive." *As well as less needy*, I thought.

"You're a sweet rose, Sarah." He folded his arms. "A great budding writer. And my best friend."

I turned slowly away from him. I headed out toward the roadway, pausing when I reached the edge of his front lawn and listened to the sound of his door gently closing, as well as the soothing silence that followed.

Chapter 12

I awkwardly stood in the center of the pet shop, looking around and pretending I was a customer waiting for service. I was surprised to see no one at the counter guarding the cash register, and no one taking care of any of the animals.

After a few minutes had passed, I walked toward an office. I knocked lightly on the closed door and quietly waited for a response.

The door was thrust open, its corner just barely missing my shoulder. Brian stood on the other side of the doorway with an annoyed look on his face.

"Brian." I stepped away from him cautiously.

"Sarah... How did you get in here?"

"Huh?"

"Store hours are nine to five," he said, mechanically. "It's eight-thirty."

"But the door was open," I said.

He placed his hand over his face. "I forgot to lock it after I came in." He leaned his body against the rim of the door and asked, "What's up?"

"I just wanted to know about what we discussed the last time I was here... the job?"

He placed his fingers against his lips. "I told you to come back in a couple of *weeks*, not a couple of *days*."

"Uh-huh," I said. "Sorry." I wasn't quite sure what species of bug had crawled up his behind, but I assumed that it must have had some fierce antennas.

"No, it's OK," he said, redeeming himself just in time before I was tempted to push the bug further up there with my foot. He walked back into his office and poured himself a cup of coffee. "You're just catching me at a bad time right now." He accidentally put too much pressure on the rim of his Styrofoam cup and spilled hot black coffee all over his white shirt.

"Damn it!" he yelled.

"Do you want a towel, or something?" I asked, looking frantically around myself.

"I don't believe this!" he shouted. He dabbed his shirt with the edge of a paper napkin. "Now I gotta go through the whole day like this!"

"Brian... I'm gonna go. This is my fault. Here I am bugging you, and it's so early in the morning."

"No, no Sarah. It's me. Trust me," he said. "I'm a mess."

"What's wrong?"

He angrily threw the moistened paper napkin into a trash can and let his hands drop to his sides. "My girlfriend broke up with me last night."

"Oh, I'm sorry," I said.

"It came completely out of left field," he said. He swept his hand over the dark brown stain on his shirt. "She's getting back together with her ex-boyfriend."

"I think it's easier when there are signs," I said. "At least you have a chance to protect yourself."

"I mean, when you've been with the same person for so many years, and you're so happy to have found that person, and you think that person is so happy to have found you. You just assume the person is the one. You get comfortable with the idea, you know? Dawn and I..." He shook his head.

I nodded sympathetically, even though I personally had never been with anyone long enough to really know what he was talking about. Then I noticed him staring at me thoughtfully.

"Wait a second," he said. "I don't know why I didn't make the connection sooner."

"What connection?"

"Dawn! Dawn Carpino. Didn't you two used to be friends? In elementary school? Junior high? I completely forgot about that."

"Dawn?" I asked.

"Yeah..."

I blinked hard. "She was my best friend." She was also one of the few remaining living people on the planet that didn't appear to use Facebook, which lowered the chances of us reuniting to nil.

He tugged at the collar of his shirt.

"I didn't even know she was living here now," I said. "So she never mentions me?"

"Hmmm?"

"Nothing." I turned away from him and started to walk toward the cash register.

"Can you believe her timing? Her mother's birthday's coming up and she and I were going to throw a big surprise party for her." He hung his head and walked slowly past me.

I watched him nervously lift a stack of requisitions off the counter and spill them all over the floor. I bent down to help him pick them up. "I'll be back... in a few *weeks*..."

"No problem," he said. "Look, I don't mean to be so noncommittal about this..."

"I understand."

He paused briefly and pointed his finger stiffly at me. "You *will* be hired. OK? If you really want to work here, it's just a matter of *when* I can officially take you on. There are a few things I have to check out first."

I smiled at him and pointed my body toward the front entrance.

"And Sarah?"

I turned back around to face him.

"If you talk to Dawn, try not to describe me as pathetic."

"Time heals, Brian," I said as I walked toward the shop entrance.

Chapter 13

I worked another lonely shift at the diner. Pamela and I stayed glued to our private stations, not saying a word to each other or looking into each other's eyes. I decided not to forgo another midday meal to avoid her company. I pushed my way through the kitchen and poured myself a cup of lentil soup. Pamela looked up at me when I entered the storage room and took a seat on a crate across from her.

I finished my lunch and headed into the main room of the diner. She stood up and followed closely behind me through the kitchen. She tapped my shoulder lightly when I bent over a table to pick up a moist rag.

I quickly twisted around and looked at her, surprised at the sudden contact.

"Shhh... Just shhh..." she whispered, even though I didn't say anything. She tousled her hair, swung her head back, and walked away.

I watched the sky turn a soft orange as the sun started to set and my long day drew to a close. The sound of the front entrance chiming jerked me awake. I watched as Gary walked inside the diner.

"Where's Pamela?" he asked.

"In the kitchen talking to one of the cooks," I said.

"Thanks for opening your mouth, by the way."

I gave him a puzzled look. Although I knew exactly what he was talking about.

"Had to say something, didn't you?"

"What?" I asked. Playing dumb.

"Don't, Sarah."

"Don't what?" Still playing dumb.

"Don't... be this way," he said, holding his finger up to my face. "I don't know what's happened to you. Haven't the slightest clue."

I looked away from him.

He started to angrily pace back and forth, staring hard into the floor. "I was up half the night with her on the phone. Why I said anything to you and actually trusted you'd keep it to yourself, I have no idea."

I lifted a stack of menus off a table and made their edges flush. "I'm sorry."

He gave me a deadpan look. "Stay out of my life."

I folded my arms and silently stared out the window at the darkening auburn sky. All of the anger I had been unleashing was like paint being splattered on a canvas, sloppily covering everything with no form, no direction. And much of it was rebounding. Was it helping me to overcome my feelings about Gary? About Pamela? About myself?

Gary strained to see beyond the small square windows of the swinging kitchen doors. He looked nervous as he stood there, glancing momentarily at his watch and then back again at the kitchen.

Pamela bounded through the kitchen doors and carelessly slammed the edge of one of them into my shoulder as she ran toward Gary.

"Thanks for waiting!" she called to him. She slipped her arm around his waist and pushed the front door open.

"It's pretty windy out there... and cold," he said to her on their way out. "But we can keep each other warm. And we have this," he boasted, holding up a bottle of wine.

"Perfect," she said, her voice muffled by the closing of the heavy glass door.

I stepped outside and watched as they melted together in a tight embrace along the roadside. I saw them move slightly apart and begin walking with their arms around each other's backside. I swallowed hard and willed any hurt and confusion I was feeling to go away. There was nothing my hurt and confusion could possibly add, except more... hurt and confusion. And something told me, despite appearances, Gary and Pamela had more than their fair share to deal with already.

I suddenly saw a shadow dart out of a batch of trees lining a small patch of road behind them. I watched as the shadow moved closer to where they walked. Looking more closely, I could see it was a man. It was Doug.

I quietly crept along the roadside, staying a distance behind them. I wasn't quite sure why or when stalking and voyeurism had become such a central theme in my life and the lives of those I was hanging out with these days. But somehow it had turned into the ultimate, shameless pastime.

Pamela and Gary talked and laughed amongst themselves, pausing occasionally to capture each other's gaze and nuzzle their noses in the napes of each other's affection. Once they reached the ravine, they moved easily down the path leading to the tranquil, black water. They stepped onto the center of the first flattened rock they came across. Pamela removed a button down sweater she was wearing. Gary slipped off his shirt.

Doug took a seat dangerously near to them, locking his arms around his knees and watching them like they were actors on a stage. He lifted the collar of his black wool coat over the loose strands of hair that framed his cheeks. I stood as still as I could in the middle of the footpath, my presence lost in the rustling noises of leaves and branches stirred up by the evening's breezes.

Gary slipped his fingers through Pamela's hair. She pulled him close to her, wrapping her bony arms around his neck and moving her fingers up and down his spine.

I saw him suddenly draw away from her.

"What's wrong?" I heard her say.

"I don't know." He pulled further away from her.

"Gary?" she asked.

He was quiet. He kept his distance from her.

"Gary, what's wrong?" she asked again.

He buried his head in his hands and continued to stay silent.

Doug stood up and took heavy, carefree steps toward the rock where the two of them sat. He walked around them and skipped over more flattened stones toward the woods on the other side of the water. He had Pamela's discarded sweater and Gary's shirt in his hand.

"Hey!" Gary shouted.

Doug smiled broadly at him. He tossed the sweater and shirt on a heap of crusty, burnt twigs, cinders, and ashes left over from previously kindled campfires. He swiftly threw chunks of fresh wood on top of them, tossed a lit match over them, and watched with vengeful glee as a small blaze erupted.

Gary pulled Pamela up by the hand and shielded her. She pushed past him and sprinted off the rock. She headed toward a thicket of trees not far from where I was crouched among fallen leaves and long, prickly branches.

I sat for a long time, peering from a distance at the two men, one shirtless and trembling from the cold, the other still and solid. Doug stared silently into the woods as Gary circled him, drawing closer with every step like he was ready to rumble. Smoke from the fire drifted past Gary's naked shoulders and brushed against the collar of Doug's coat. I watched closely as he continued to side-step around Doug. He kept moving, the muscles in his neck rolling under his skin and forming surreal shadows in the firelight. Doug slowly moved his hand toward his chest and began to unbutton his coat. He slipped it off his shoulders and, continuing to stare ahead of himself, draped it over Gary's shoulders in the smoky air.

"This isn't about you," Doug said to him.

Pamela darted out of the woods and charged at Gary, pushing him off the rock. She swung her body around and faced Doug. "Is this revenge?"

Doug stepped toward her and brought his face inches away from hers. "You ruined my life," he said.

"Oh, please," she moaned. "It was an accident."

"Like this?" He pushed her.

"It was an *accident*," she said again.

"Yeah, an accident. Like this." He pushed her again.

"Stop it!" She pushed him back.

He shoved her more forcefully, causing her to stumble near the fire. A flame attached itself to the cuff of her blue jeans and flashed brightly. Trying to stomp the fire out, her foot slid across moss-covered stones in the surrounding water. She fell backward, her head hitting the hard rock beneath her.

Doug slowly knelt down and held Pamela's head still in his hands. His shadow darkened the smooth shine of her skin in the firelight.

Gary's face grew white as he bent down and placed his hand on Pamela's forehead. Still clad in Doug's long, black coat, he lightly placed his cheek against her rising and falling stomach. "Pamela..." he whispered. She drew a deep breath and exhaled. Gary lifted his head up off of her and rested his fingertips gently on her rib cage.

Doug stood up. He pulled a cigarette out of a pack in his tattered shirt pocket and lit it.

"Where's my boyfriend?" Pamela suddenly asked in a weary voice.

"What?" Gary said. "I'm here."

"Where's my boyfriend?" she asked again.

"I said I'm here." Gary leaned his head closer to her.

"No. Dougie," Pamela moaned.

Doug stopped smoking and looked at her, his mouth twisted as though he had eaten something bitter. "What's she saying?"

"Dougie," she groaned. "I need you."

Doug cocked his head and looked up at the sky. He threw his old cigarette on the ground, smoothed a new one out and tapped it against his hands. He lit it, tilted his head back and blew a stream of smoke up in the air. He sucked hard on the end of his cigarette and blew another cloud of smoke out in front of himself. Then he stood quietly, staring down at her.

Gary stood up and pulled Doug away from her by the arm. "Just answer her," he said. "Go with it. Must have something to do with the fall."

"I'm not going to go with anything!" Doug said, incredulously. "What's she even talking about?"

"You could be charged," Gary whispered. "For assault."

"She lost her balance," Doug whispered back. "It was an accident."

"You pushed her." Gary let go of Doug's arm. "You pushed her, and then she lost her balance."

Doug was quiet.

"Dougie..." Pamela said. "Dougie, please come here." She slowly sat up on the rock and lightly blew air from her mouth into cupped hands. "I'm so cold..." She stood up and clung to Doug's arm, resting her head on his shoulder. Her eyes suddenly looked glossy and woeful. "Dougie..." she said.

His mouth contorted again. Crevices formed in his forehead as he walked away from her.

"Everything OK, Dougie?" she asked, walking toward him.

"Yeah, yeah..." he muttered, looking helplessly at Gary.

She smiled, clinging to his arm again. "I know this is going to sound kind of crazy, but I feel like celebrating."

"Celebrating *what*?" Doug asked, bewildered.

She chuckled softly and pinched his forearm. "Life!" she said, giddily, slipping her arm once again around his and rubbing her forehead against his cheek. She then brought her face only inches away from his and stared at him with glistening eyes.

"You're nuts," he mumbled. He pulled his arm out of her grasp and took a few steps away from her. He knelt down on the ground.

A chilly wind swept past and teased the moonlit water.

"Dougie..." Pamela whined. "I was hoping..." she said, placing her hand on his knee and leaning toward him, "...that maybe we could get some wine."

"Don't touch me there." He lifted her hand off his knee and set it down on her own. "Look." He pointed to the bottle of white burgundy wine resting against a large fallen branch that Gary had placed there earlier. "You don't remember bringing that?"

"Unbelievable!" she shrieked, clapping her hands.

"Go ahead. Help yourself," he said. "Actually... Never mind." He unscrewed the cap of the wine bottle and stared at it for a long time. "I shouldn't be doing this," he mumbled, swirling the liquid in the bottle a few times before lifting it to his mouth. He tipped it so that the wine flowed fast and quickly gulped it down.

"Why do you have to drink so much?" she asked.

"So I can be conscious of so little," he snarled, handing it to her.

"No..." she said. She pushed it away and tugged at his shirt sleeve. "Give me this. I'm cold."

"My shirt?" he asked.

"I think it will fit me," she said. As she tried to pull his shirt off of him, he hunched his shoulders and moved his arms in such a way that made it impossible for her to remove it.

"This is how you're gonna treat me?" she asked in a teary voice, a look of dejection in her eyes.

"Ask me," he said. "Just *ask* me for my shirt. Can you do that? Do you know how?" He sighed heavily and slipped the shirt off his shoulders and arms. He folded it into a messy ball and threw it at her.

She looked at him, hugging the shirt tightly against her body and not saying anything. Then she eased her way into the marginal warmth of the garment, sat solemnly on a rock, and whispered, "Thanks."

He took another long drink of the wine and stared down at her. "Knock it off, will you?" he growled.

"What?" she asked.

"This little act you're putting on."

"What act?"

He drank a little more wine and spit into the water. He tilted the wine bottle to his lips again and let it flow into his mouth and down his throat.

"Dougie, I love you," she said softly. "You know that, don't you?"

He looked at her for a long time, his back bent and his hand frozen in place around the nearly empty wine bottle. He slowly lifted it up and handed it to her. "Here. There's still some left."

"Thanks, honey," she said, smiling a fatigued smile.

Doug belched loudly and stood up. "This is a great night, isn't it?"

Pamela cocked her head and looked up at the sky. "It's funny how on cloudy nights the sky looks... almost touchable. Doesn't it? I can see all the clouds so clearly... especially the ones surrounding the moon." She sipped some wine and started to hiccup.

"You can't tell me you're drunk," Doug said, swaying slightly from side to side, noticeably trying to keep his balance.

"I'm a lightweight," she said, chuckling.

"Yeah? Well so am I..." Doug slurred.

Pamela stood up and stepped toward him. "Sure you are, Dougie."

"It's all muscle," he groaned.

She stared deeply into his eyes and placed her hand over his bare stomach. He jerked his body away from her, stumbled over his feet and fell on the large stone beneath him. Laughing, Pamela held her hand out to him.

"Could we go up there?" she asked. She pointed to a lofty precipice that looked out over the town's twisting roadways and cottages.

"What's up there that we can't get from down here?" Doug asked.

"The sky," she said, smirking at him and batting her eyelashes.

"You're twisted."

"Twisted or not, I want to go up there," she said. She started climbing up a natural staircase of staggered flat sandstones that snaked around trees and brush and led to the very top of the cliff. Doug reluctantly followed, swaying and periodically losing his balance, yet trailing closely behind her. Gary wavered, seeming as though he would also follow the procession. Yet he finally turned away and headed toward the path that led out to the main roadway, taking Doug's coat with him. I watched Doug and Pamela until I couldn't see either. I then began my own quiet ascent toward the top of the precipice.

Once at the top of the path, Pamela folded her arms. A cold wind blowing past her, she buried her chin in Doug's shirt. It hung loosely over her thin frame.

"This isn't fair," Doug whined. "I'm freezing." He slapped his hands on his naked chest and rib cage.

"Do jumping jacks," Pamela said. "Exercise. Move around. Get that circulation going."

"Take a hike," he growled. "And give me back my shirt."

"No," she pouted. "I'm not feeling well."

"It was your idea to stay out here, to come up here," he said. He kicked some dirt and started to pace.

"I have an idea," Pamela said. She slowly sat down on a rotting log and rocked back and forth. "Try walking on your hands, Dougie. Just like I taught you."

"I can barely walk on my feet right now," he said.

"Then it will be a true challenge." She softly blew into her cupped hands and rubbed them fast.

"Oh just... give me my shirt." He stretched his arm out toward her.

She wrapped herself more tightly. "Walk on your hands."

"Then you'll give me back my shirt?" he asked.

She nodded.

"And we can get out of here?"

She nodded again.

He stood in place and quietly stared at her. A gust of wind suddenly made him shiver, and he crossed his arms across his bare chest. "You're out of your mind," he said, suddenly. "I'm not going to walk on my damn hands. This is nuts."

"Then no shirt," Pamela said. "And we stay here even longer."

Another gale knocked him back a few steps. He shook his head and looked down at the ground. "I don't even... know if I remember how," he said. He rubbed his hands together.

"You never forget," she reassured him.

He placed his hands on the ground and kicked his feet up toward the night sky. He kept his legs suspended in the air over his head for around a half a second before he lost his balance and tumbled forward. Laughing, he said, "Even if I was sober, there's no way."

"Yes there is," Pamela coached. "It just takes some practice after you haven't done it for a long time. Try again."

Still lying flat on his back, he turned his head and raised his eyes at her. "Then I'll get my shirt back?"

"Yes," she said, smiling weakly.

He groaned and rolled himself to his feet. Standing, he pressed his hand on his forehead. "I'm real dizzy."

"Like I told you before," Pamela said. "It makes it more of a challenge."

He shook his head and started rubbing his hands together again. He took three unsteady steps forward, leaned toward the ground, and kicked his legs up in the air. He lingered with his knees bent and hanging over his head for a few seconds, and then he moved one hand in front of the other. He started laughing after he took two steps with his hands and tumbled over.

Pamela clapped her hands. "You did it! Try it again!"

"No," he said. "The shirt's mine. Hand it over."

"Just once more?" she begged. "Try to stay up a little longer."

"Why?" he asked, lying on the ground and rubbing his forehead.

She sighed. "Doesn't it feel good to have all that blood pumping?"

He blew a stream of air out of his mouth and started snickering.

"What are you laughing at?" she asked.

"You," he said, still snickering.

"What?"

"Nothin'," he said, slowly standing and running his fingers through his hair. He kicked his way into another handstand, this time moving his palms against the ground steadily and gracefully. He carried all of his weight on his hands across the ground and said, in between large gulps of chilly air, "I'll... always... be... an... athlete..." There was a look of intensity on his face as he moved one hand in front of the other, staunchly distancing himself from Pamela.

She watched him approach the cliff's edge. She stood up then and called out to him, "Stop, you idiot! You go any further and that'll be it!"

I saw him grip his hands around the very edge of the precipice and begin to lower his legs to the ground.

"Hope that gave you a good scare, though," she said, smiling.

Suddenly he lost his balance. His body flipped over the edge of the cliff. He clung tenaciously to a pointed slab of slate jutting out.

"Doug!" I screamed, rushing toward him. I could see Pamela's posture change again in my periphery as I grabbed his arm with my hand and tried pulling his weight up onto the ledge of the cliff. He soundlessly dangled over large, jagged rocks and treacherous shoals forty or so feet below him. "Give me your hand," I said, exasperated.

Breathing heavily, he stared up at me. "Sarah?"

"Yes, it's me," I said. "I'm here."

"Sarah?" he said again.

"Yes, Doug..."

"Why should I give you my hand?" he asked.

I looked down at him. "What do you mean?"

"I mean," he said. "What's waiting for me up there?"

"The rest of your life," I said, without hesitation.

He spit down toward the gravelly rocks below him. He hung his head down and pressed his chin against his chest. "The rest of my life." He spit again toward the far away ground and repeated, "The rest of my life..."

"Doug..." I said.

"My... life." He spit once more into the air and moved toward the barbed end of the projecting rock. "The rest of... my... life."

I bent down and reached for his arm again. "Tortured souls never rest," I said, almost as though Scott was whispering in my ear and coaching me to say it. I placed my hand on his arm and gently eased my fingers around it.

He bowed his head and looked below him into the darkness.

I squeezed his arm hard and pulled on it with as much strength as I could muster. I was surprised to feel Pamela's fingers clawing into my waist as she tried to pull both myself and Doug away from the cliff's edge. I wondered if he could feel her tugging on us as well. And I wondered if it meant anything to him if he could.

"Doug..." I said.

He looked up at me.

"Doug..." I said again.

He continued to look at me. He stared into my eyes.

"I love you," I heard myself suddenly saying. My voice was accompanied by the sound of the wind rustling leaves and moving branches. I tried to look beyond where he was hanging but could only see pitch black darkness that seemed to go on forever.

Doug continued to gaze at me. He slowly started to pull himself up over the edge of the precipice using nothing but the strength in his arms. He dragged his body onto me, and we both rested together on the flat ground beneath us.

Pamela backed away. I could see the paths of tears that had run down her cheeks and a blanket of moisture covering her upper lip. She turned her head and walked to a large, fallen branch. She knelt down in front of it and stared at the ground.

Doug lifted his head off of my chest and looked up at me. He reached for my hair and lightly touched it.

A funnel of dry, brown, and orange sugar maple leaves formed on the ground and drifted toward the dirt and pebbles at Pamela's feet. I watched her fall back onto a patch of brown, withered grass and pull her knees close to her chest. A sheet of water sparkling in the moonlight blanketed her cheeks. She lowered her forehead into the palm of her hand, looking a little like a scolded kitten on the verge of licking its invisible wounds.

I slowly sat up, swiping at the dirt and crusty leaves that clung to my clothes and gradually relieving myself of the weight of Doug's body on my hips and legs. Looking down at his large, bare arms, I noticed goose bumps.

"He needs his shirt," I said, reaching my hand out toward Pamela.

She stared at me. "What are you doing here?" she asked.

I continued to keep my arm and hand outstretched, without answering her.

She slowly lifted Doug's shirt over her arms and head. She threw it in a tight, twisted ball in my direction. It landed on the ground near my feet.

"You've taken enough from him," I said, breaking the silence.

"And what do you know," she said, "about what I've taken from him?"

I knelt down and lifted Doug's shirt, holding it tightly in my fist. "It's the same thing that you've taken from me," I said. "Pride." I loosened my grip on his shirt and smoothed out its wrinkles as I pressed it against my body.

"Oh, give me a break," she said with disgust. "Your weakness and his weakness aren't my problem. Neither is anybody's lack of *pride.* Own it."

I gently handed Doug's shirt to him. He slowly sat upright and lethargically pulled the tattered garment over his head. He lowered himself back toward the ground and began to drift off to sleep, breathing deeply and loudly into a large clump of dead leaves beneath his cheek.

"You're right," I said, turning to face Pamela.

"I know I'm right." She smiled smugly.

"I've gone my whole life feeling like I don't measure up. Because of you. Because of people like you," I said. "And because of it, I've let a lot of bad things happen. Maybe I've even brought a lot of those things on."

Pamela placed her hand on the back of her neck and dragged it toward her cheek. She then leaned her head

thoughtfully into it. She nodded as though in agreement.
She started to stand.

"We're all responsible for ourselves, and our actions,"
I said, my eyes meeting hers. "All of us are responsible.
And that includes you."

She crossed her arms and looked at me, saying
nothing. She continued looking at me for a long time
without blinking. I kept expecting her to say something, yet
her lips did not so much as quiver.

"*That... includes... you,*" I repeated, more slowly. I
shifted my gaze to the highest branches of a group of
billowing oaks, their stance rigid against the deep lavender
sky despite the forceful evening winds.

"You don't know anything about me."

"I know you think you're a stronger person than me," I
said.

"I *know* I'm a stronger person than you."

I rocked my foot back and forth on the ground. "Have
you ever been hurt by anybody?" I asked. "I mean, have
you ever allowed anybody to *affect* you?"

"To affect me?"

"Yeah," I said. "To influence you. To make you doubt
yourself. Or maybe not even like yourself."

"Come on," she mumbled. "You must think I'm pretty
stupid."

"What do you mean?" I asked.

"I'm not going to get roped into this role-reversal
garbage of yours."

"It's not garbage," I said. "I just want to talk to you. Can you do that?"

"Not likely," she said, shaking her head. "Look, Sarah. I *know* I hurt you."

I looked up at her briefly, and then lowered my eyes back toward my sneakers.

"And of course I know what it feels like to get hurt," she said. "I'm a human being, aren't I?"

I remained silent.

"But there's a big difference between you and me," she said. "I make sure that whoever it was who hurt me is *never able to hurt me again.* You *let it happen over and over.* And you know what?"

"No. What?" I asked.

"I really can't stand that about you," she said.

My cheeks grew very hot. I lowered my head as far down as I could toward the ground so she would not be able to see my face.

"You know what else?" she asked.

"Mmm?" I mumbled.

"It makes me want to hurt you even more."

I glanced up at her, half-expecting to see a mischievous smile on her face. Yet her expression was dark and serious. I drew a deep breath, and exhaled slowly. "Why can't you just accept the fact that I'm different from you? And leave it at that?"

"You're a wimp," she said. "I can't understand how anybody can go through life the way you do."

217

"Or Doug," I said. I squinted and rocked my finger at her.

She squatted back on the ground. "He's such a weak person," she said, shaking her head. "I knew him back when we were kids. I know you knew him, too."

I looked at her.

"You used to go fishing together. I'd see you two all the time here."

"You did?" I asked, although I already had my suspicion. Still, my face flushed. So it really was her, quietly watching us, hidden in the woods. I pictured her wanting to be the one Doug was teaching how to fish. The one Doug was talking to. The one Doug was holding. I pictured her achingly and bitterly accepting that I had something she did not. And I pictured it killing her.

She hesitantly looked up at me. "How much do you know about him? About me and him?"

"I know about a fall he took," I said. "A fall he was forced to take that changed his life."

She slowly rose to her feet and growled, "That was an *accident*."

I started to walk away from her in the moonlit darkness. I gradually came to a stop and turned back around to face her. "Is anything really an accident with you?" I asked. "You poached just about everyone you know I've been close to. Doug... Gary... What's that about?"

"They came to *me*," she said. "It had nothing to do with you."

I quietly stood and nodded my head, my movements slow and exaggerated. I didn't believe her, and I wanted her to know it. I swiveled around and began heading away.

Suddenly, I heard a clattering, a shuffling. When I turned, I saw it was Pamela. She was lying on the ground, a shallow ditch underneath her. The uneven ground, veiled by darkness, had caused her to stumble and fall. She was lying fetus-like clutching her knee and sobbing.

"What happened?" I asked.

"I must've... lost my balance... somehow. I can't see... It's dark." Water gushed from her eyes as she moaned and rocked her body back and forth. "My knee!" she screamed.

"This is turning out to be a dangerous night for you." I slowly backed away from her.

"I lost my balance!" she yelled, as tears streamed down her face.

"*You*?" I asked. "Lost your balance?"

"There's all this *crap* lying around here! There are all these rocks and pebbles... and tree roots..."

I started to walk away from her again.

"Where are you going!" she yelled. "I think I twisted... It feels like I *broke* my leg! I can't move it! I can't walk!"

I pivoted on a jagged rock. "Why don't you try walking on your hands?"

"Get over here!" she hollered. Still clutching her knee with one hand, she reached the other hand out to me. "Can you help me get back down the path? To the ravine?" She kept her arm suspended in the air and continued to grasp at the empty space around her for a long time. Finally, she let it drop hard against the ground and breathlessly said, "I can't... believe you're acting this way. I have... no one here besides you who can... help me."

I began descending the footpath leading down the precipice. I turned toward her and said, "You don't need anybody, do you?"

She wrinkled her brow and pressed her cheek against the ground.

"You're a strong person," I said.

"Could you please just... help me?" she asked, wearily.

I leaned toward her. "Are you trying to tell me that you're not strong enough to cope with this on your own?"

Wincing and moaning, she brought her chin in toward her chest.

"Pamela?"

She moaned louder.

I took a few deep breaths of the chilly, autumn air and walked back toward her. *Hurting people hurt people*, I thought to myself, the phrase suddenly coming back to me from a church sermon from long ago. I lifted her up off the ground and let her lean her weight against me as I carried her down the path, past the ravine, and toward the main roadway. We emerged from the brush. I gently set her down against an old, weathered mile marker sticking out of a patch of withered grass. She slowly lowered her chest to the ground and rounded her body up into a tight ball.

"Are you feeling any pain?" I asked.

Sobbing, she brought her knee in closer to her chest.

"Are you?" I asked again.

She opened her eyes to form narrow slits and stared at the mile marker.

I sighed heavily. "Can you admit that you feel it?"

"What?" she asked, her lips taut.

"Pain," I said.

She angrily stared up at me. She tightly closed her eyes and groaned. "Of course I feel pain! What's your problem?"

"I'm not talking about the kind you can take an aspirin for," I said.

She clutched her leg, rocking her body back and forth, and keeping her mouth tightly closed. Her face turned a deep purplish color and her chin became filled with lines and indentations. She opened her eyes wide and slowly shifted her gaze up toward me. She forced her quivering mouth open and suddenly screamed, "What do you want from me!"

"I want to understand you," I said. Another sermon came to mind. The pastor was telling the congregation about icebergs in the ocean, and how the part of them that we see jutting out of the water is only around ten percent, and the remaining ninety percent is submerged and invisible. He then pointed out that the Titanic didn't sink from the ten percent that could be seen, but rather from the ninety percent that couldn't be seen.

Pamela stared at my chin, glancing only briefly at my eyes, and then lowered her gaze to my throat.

"I want to understand why you have this need to hurt people," I said.

She blinked hard, still staring at my throat.

"Like Doug," I said. *Like me.*

Her eyes narrowed and water squeezed out of their corners. "Quit playing little analyst," she said, breathlessly. "You have no clue, so don't even bother to try."

"He had a future," I said. "In football."

Tears fell from the edge of her cheek and dropped to the ground. She continued to stare only at my throat.

"Why did you hurt him, Pamela? Why did you push him?" I asked. "Why did you make him fall?"

She opened her eyes slowly. A surge of water escaped down her cheeks. A small patch of ground below her was starting to turn muddy as more tears dripped down onto it. She pressed her forehead into the cold, wet earth and pushed hard into the soil with it. She looked up at me then, her eyes sad and watery. Her lips moved slightly, like she wanted to say something. Instead, she just continued to silently gaze at me.

"Why did you hurt him?" I asked her again.

She turned her head so that her ear was touching the dirt below her, and she stared at my mouth. Lifting her head up off the ground, she looked into my eyes. "Doug

222

had told me that he never forgot you, never got over you." She lowered her head to the ground again and stared up at the sky, blinking up at the crescent moon. Her breathing was slow and rhythmic, almost as if she were meditating. Droplets of water continued to fall from her eyes and darken the ground beneath her. "I already knew how he felt, even without him saying that. I knew from as far back as when we were kids. When I saw a letter he had written to you, after he moved away."

I looked squarely into her eyes then, knowingly.

"Doug told me about that letter," I said. "I told him I never got it. That he sent it to the wrong address."

"I tore it up," she mumbled. "Almost hoping that by getting rid of it, it'd also get rid of his feelings. I tried to hide the evidence," she said, snorting. "So then there we were, years later, and he's telling me everything I might have already known deep down. But nothing I should have had to hear. He was with *me*. You were just a memory. I didn't deserve to be hurt like that... by him."

I gripped her shoulder tightly with my fingers, and I lowered my cheek against them, slipping into my own thoughtful gaze. "I'm not sure... things are always so simple," I said.

She stared at me.

"Take Gary."

She rolled her eyes. "I'd rather not."

I smiled at her. "Talk about complicated."

She smiled back, weakly. "Where *is* he?" she asked. "Did he go home, or what?"

I shrugged. "I saw him leaving… with Doug's coat." I started to chuckle at the image. "He just… took off with his coat. Which I guess is only fair since Doug set his shirt on fire."

"So he just left, huh?" Her smile faded, and she fell into a dead stare.

"He left…" I said. *He left with Doug's coat. And he left with a little of her. And a little of me.*

I stared up at the night sky, at the clouds, their transparent fringes filtering the glow of the moon. "We can choose who we want to love," I said, "but we really can't choose who loves us, can we?"

She nodded slowly.

"Seems like we can choose a lot of things," I said. "Doesn't mean they've been chosen for us, though." *Had to have faith. Even if the plan was different from our own, even if we didn't like it.*

"Doug broke my heart," Pamela said, suddenly. "You want me to admit that? OK. I admitted it. Doug broke my heart, and I was stupidly hoping Gary… could put it back together. I was hoping he… could just… love me back. I just needed someone to love me… back." She winced and gripped her knee. "Damn it, this hurts so badly."

I rubbed her shoulder lightly, trying to soothe her.

She looked at me then, staring fiercely. "I gave up everything after *Doug* gave up everything, OK?" She

224

closed her eyes tightly as though it would help her mind to be blind to the memory. "I quit school. I quit acting. I was so ashamed. I couldn't believe I got so out of control." She started sobbing. "It wasn't fair for me to have a shot at my dreams if he was cheated out of his."

I kept my hand cupped around her shoulder. I didn't say anything.

"So you go ahead and keep thinking whatever you want to about me." She started to cry. "That I'm some kind of monster. That I have no feelings."

"I don't think that," I said, softly.

She continued to cry.

"What I do think is that you have to stop hurting." My voice grew louder. "And so does Doug."

And so do I.

"You have to stop hurting each other," I said. "And you have to stop hurting yourselves."

"I know," she breathed, her eyes downcast.

I soon heard the crunching of dry leaves and the smacking of branches growing louder from deep within the woods. I glanced toward the start of the path leading into the ravine, and I saw Doug emerge from the thicket and plant his feet shakily on the roadside. As soon as he steadied himself, his eyes fell on Pamela.

She looked up at him as he approached us. I watched him clumsily amble toward us as well, as I stayed low to the ground near Pamela. He stood quietly, his six-foot plus frame looming over us and his shadow blocking the light a nearby street lamp had cast.

Pamela slowly reached her hand up toward him and kept her arm extended in the air. "I'm sorry, Doug," she said, quietly.

He stood motionless.

"I'm sorry," she said again, slightly more loudly, her voice strained and hoarse.

He paused, looking confused. Then he hesitantly reached down for her hand and held it in his own.

"What happened to you?" he asked.

"I fell," she said. "I hurt my leg."

He pulled her up and let her lean her body against him as she tried to stand. Then he looked at me and stretched his free hand out toward my cheek, stroking it with his thumb. I stood up and placed my hand over his.

He smiled at me. "I love you," he said.

I smiled back.

Pamela pressed more of her weight into his side and began trying to walk. I moved next to her and took her arm, encouraging her to lean on me as well. The three of us slowly started down the main roadway, away from the glow of the street lamp, away from the support of the mile marker, and away from the lure of Angel Rock Leap.

I could see Scott in the distance walking toward us, keeping himself warm in a threadbare, faded blue sweatshirt zippered to his chin. Its hood was pulled over his head.

"What happened here?" he asked, gently gripping Pamela's elbow and prying her loose from us.

"She hurt herself," I said. "She needs help walking."

Scott placed his arm around the small of her back and whispered, "Here, lean on me hon." She stared at him, longingly and gratefully, and began hobbling along the road again using his body as her crutch.

We can choose who we want to love, I thought. *But we can't choose who loves us, can we?* I watched Scott's face as he helped Pamela. His cheeks were flushed, and while he looked concerned, like a worried father taking care of a sick child, he also looked happy. And the two of them together looked like pieces of a puzzle that fit together perfectly.

Doug suddenly slipped his hand in mine and squeezed it, looking down at me and gesturing with his head for the two of us to walk alongside them. His large hand felt good around my own and gave me some much-needed warmth on a far too chilly night.

I closed my eyes for a brief moment and opened them. I could see clouds swiftly moving and patches of black sky emerging from behind them.

We continued to slowly walk together. I quietly listened to the sounds of the night and felt the chill of the autumn air against my neck. The further we traveled along the roadside, the clearer it became that there was only one direction for us to go.

Forward.

Chapter 14

I lingered near the door of Scott's bedroom, and slowly started turning the knob.

"Going so soon?" he asked.

I stopped my hand from twisting and leaned my head against the door. "I thought you and Pamela were going out tonight."

"Yeah, but we still have some time. The movie doesn't start until eight. Besides, she's at an audition. Gotta wait until that's over." He stood up from the chair he was sitting on and adjusted his pajama bottoms. He closed his robe and tightened its belt. "I just have to take a shower before she gets here, but I can do that real quick."

I nodded. "Maybe I can convince Doug to take me out somewhere tonight," I said. "Brian told me I don't have to be in until noon tomorrow and can sleep in late in the morning. And Doug's been studying all day and could really use a break."

"How's that program going for him? Does he have a long time to go, or what?"

"He's on his way," I said. "A lot of his college credits transferred, which is making it so much easier for him. At some point, he'll have to pass an exam for a license. He really wants this."

"I heard you could make over 80,000 dollars as a physical therapist," Scott said. "He'll join the ranks of the country's elitists. Money is power. Power is control."

I started walking back toward him. "I'm writing a book," I said. "I started it yesterday, and I'm going to try to finish it in the next year or so and get it published."

"A book? Seriously?" He flopped his body on his bed and turned to face me, his head resting on his hand, his elbow pressed into his comforter. "What's it about?"

"I have the synopsis with me," I said. "Want me to read it to you?"

"Absolutely," he said.

I rested my purse on the edge of his desk and started rummaging through it. "Here it is." I lifted a piece of paper up and said, "I'm calling it 'Angel Rock Leap.'"

He smiled.

"Ill-fated circumstances lead 19 year-old Tara away from New England and back to her hometown in Upstate New York," I said, pausing to look into his eyes for dramatic effect.

His smile broadened. "Awesome," he said. "Hey, how about have Tara become a lightning rod for crap? Maybe an apartment fire, a fall with minor injuries, a theft. A hamster suicide. She is brought low. She might reek of smoke from the apartment fire or she might continually pour coffee on herself as a result of the thumb she dislocates in a fall."

"Why don't you shut up and let me finish?" I said, continuing. "Tara finds life in the otherwise quiet hamlet of Palenville to be unsettling, as she is continuously reminded of unpleasant childhood memories involving her high school nemesis, Patricia, and her ex-boyfriend, Barry. Tara tries unsuccessfully to get Patricia to apologize for her cruelty when they were school mates, and she is deflated by Barry's indifference toward her when the two first reunite. She is also faced with the disturbing discovery that Barry and Patricia share a complex romantic relationship."

Scott put his finger up in the air and interrupted. "How about you have Tara placing the cause of her problem with Patricia as her failure to have done high school 'right'? Or perhaps, Tara figures she screwed up by taking high school so seriously by skipping social events, by cowering with books instead of hanging out with friends, because it got her nowhere and nothing... except for singed hair and a dead hamster and shoes with chemical burns in them."

I grabbed his finger, which was still in the air, and forcefully lowered it. "Scott, please? This is *my* moment?"

"A lot of famous authors have ghost writers, Sarah," he said.

"Adding to Tara's distress," I continued, ignoring him, "are strange incidences that lead her to believe that she is being watched or followed. Tara's instincts prove to be correct when an ominous stranger, menacing and eccentric, surprisingly reveals himself to be Dave, Tara's first love from childhood. Tara's happiest memories are of the days she and Dave, only twelve at the time, had spent together at the popular local ravine, Angel Rock Leap. Disheveled and lost, the vagabond and older Dave is at first unrecognizable to Tara.

"Dave looks to Tara, a symbol of purity and innocence, for comfort. He comes back into Tara's life broken, having had a promising career in football cut short years earlier by an injury accidentally inflicted on him by Patricia, with whom he had a brief, but serious, relationship. Similar to Tara, Dave cannot suppress his anger and resentment toward Patricia, and blames her for ruining his life.

"The back and forth exchanges between Dave and Patricia culminate in one final dangerous act of deception that almost brings more irreparable harm to Dave. Tara's encouraging words and gestures of love and caring bring him to safety. The incidence forces Tara and Patricia to talk openly and honestly, a conversation that reveals a source of pain and sorrow shared by both that serves to bring them closer.

"The triangle between Dave, Patricia, and Tara transitions from discord to harmony as each learns to accept the faults in each other, and to recognize and appreciate the faults in themselves. This is a coming of age story in which adversity turns out to be the healing remedy for three people whose inability to let go of the past has prevented them from moving forward toward the future." I lowered the piece of paper to my waistline. "That's all I have so far."

Scott stared at me for a few seconds in silence. He drew a deep breath and exhaled slowly. "Sarah?"

"Yes? What did you think?" I asked.

"Now that... is my kind of story," he said. "Just one problem with it. Well, actually, *two* problems with it."

"Yeah? What's that?"

"First of all, where's Skippy?" he asked.

"Huh? Who's Skippy?"

He grinned.

I laughed. "Skippy. Of course. Well, Skippy is kind of... larger than life, you know? A guru... with so much power and influence as to almost be Svengali-like. So difficult to tame Skippy to character proportions," I said. "I just... couldn't box Skippy and all his omnipotence in like that. I hope you understand."

He nodded. "Yes, yes, I do see what you mean. OK... I understand. Totally. I was a little put off there by the word 'triangle' as opposed to 'quadrangle', but I get it now. If anything, Skippy would probably end up making it more of a trapezoid or a rhombus or a perpendicular line segment. And who needs that kind of complexity in a story that's supposed to be just feel-good fluff?"

I pretended to wipe invisible beads of sweat off of my forehead and let out a sigh of fake relief. "So what's the other problem with it?" I asked.

He belched loudly, pretended to catch it with his hand, and blew it in my direction. "Not gassy enough."

Acknowledgements

Special thanks to Kelly Gousios and Dave Gracer, for their invaluable suggestions and input. Thanks to Frank Williams for his contributions. And many thanks to Kenny Colville, for always inspiring.

Author Bios

Ellen Weisberg is a cancer researcher at
the Dana Farber Cancer Institute and
Principal Associate in Medicine at Harvard
Medical School (Boston, MA), with a
doctorate in pharmacology. Ken Yoffe is a
pediatrician (Billerica, MA). He also holds
a doctorate in genetics.

Publications include short stories and
poetry published in *PKA's Advocate*
(bimonthly literary publication), *The
Writing Disorder* (quarterly online literary
journal and print anthology book), and
Natural Solutions (holistic health
magazine). They have also published six
children's books (Galde Press and
Chipmunkapublishing) and one young
adult novel (Chipmunkapublishing).

They perform as part of a circus troupe that promotes
bullying awareness to Boys and Girls Clubs, retirement
homes, and nursing homes throughout New England. The
anti-bullying children's fantasy, *Fruit of the Vine*
(Chipmunkapublishing, 2010), is being used as part of this
show.
Ellen and Ken live in Chelmsford, MA, with their 10 year-
old daughter, Emily.